The moment of truth

"Ready?" her father asked.

Jacobs nodded and placed his hands carefully under the corpse's shoulders while Justin put his hands beneath her hip. Her father held the head.

"One, two, three!" Patrick said. "Careful, now."

The body was stiff, in full rigor, and as it rolled the hair fell forward to cover the face in a chestnut-colored web; gently, her father removed it, and then his eyes grew wide. "Oh, no," he said. "Oh, God, please no."

And then Cameryn saw the perfect oval face and the eyes staring blankly, and she felt her hand fly to her mouth and tears blurred her vision until she couldn't see anymore.

● ● ●

OTHER BOOKS YOU MAY ENJOY

THE
CHRISTOPHER
KILLER

A Forensic Mystery by

Alane Ferguson

SPEAK

Published by the Penguin Group

Penguin Group (USA) Inc., 345 Hudson Street, New York, New York 10014, U.S.A.
Penguin Group (Canada), 90 Eglinton Avenue East, Suite 700,
Toronto, Ontario, Canada M4P 2Y3 (a division of Pearson Penguin Canada Inc.)
Penguin Books Ltd, 80 Strand, London WC2R 0RL, England
Penguin Ireland, 25 St Stephen's Green, Dublin 2, Ireland (a division of Penguin Books Ltd)
Penguin Group (Australia), 250 Camberwell Road, Camberwell, Victoria 3124, Australia
(a division of Pearson Australia Group Pty Ltd)
Penguin Books India Pvt Ltd, 11 Community Centre,
Panchsheel Park, New Delhi - 110 017, India
Penguin Group (NZ), 67 Apollo Drive, Rosedale, North Shore 0632, New Zealand
(a division of Pearson New Zealand Ltd)
Penguin Books (South Africa) (Pty) Ltd, 24 Sturdee Avenue,
Rosebank, Johannesburg 2196, South Africa

Registered Offices: Penguin Books Ltd, 80 Strand, London WC2R 0RL, England

First published in the United States of America by Viking,
a division of Penguin Young Readers Group, 2006
This Sleuth edition published by Speak,
an imprint of Penguin Group (USA) Inc., 2007

10 9 8 7 6 5 4 3 2 1

THE LIBRARY OF CONGRESS HAS CATALOGED THE VIKING/SLEUTH EDITION AS FOLLOWS:
Ferguson, Alane.
The Christopher killer : a forensic mystery / Alane Ferguson.
p. cm.
Summary: On the payroll as an assistant to her coroner father,
seventeen-year-old Cameryn Mahoney uses her knowledge of forensic medicine
to catch the killer of a friend while putting herself in terrible danger.
ISBN 0-670-06008-9 (hardcover)
[1. Coroners—Fiction. 2. Forensic sciences—Fiction. 3. Fathers and daughters—Fiction.
4. Mystery and detective stories.] I. Title.
PZ7.F3547Chr 2006
[Fic]—dc22 2005015806

Speak Sleuth ISBN 978-0-14-240811-7

Printed in the United States of America

Set in Bookman ITC light
Book design by Jim Hoover

To my editor, Tracy Gates—
my partner in crime

Chapter One

"YES, I CAN BE THERE in half an hour. Any idea of when he died?" Cameryn's father murmured into the telephone. He sat at the kitchen table, his legs sprawled out from the wooden chair, his thick, uncombed hair bristling from his head like roofing thatch. The pencil scratched along the yellow pad as he listened. "That long in a bathtub filled with water? There'll be a stink, then. Keep the doors and windows closed and seal off the hallway if you can."

"A floater—that doesn't sound good," Cameryn said under her breath. From her forensic books she knew only too well what water did to skin. Outside, a bird warbled from a low-hanging branch. It was strange, Cameryn thought, the way routine things kept right on going even when a death call came in to the Mahoney home. An anonymous body sat bloating in a tub of water, and yet golden Colorado sunlight still poured into their kitchen, setting fire to the orange-red flowers that lined the window ledge. The *thwick, thwick, thwick* of sprinklers blended into the hum of a distant mower, while her grandmother, whom she called "Mammaw" after the old Irish way, chopped a green pepper in cadence with the ticking of the wall clock. No matter what ugliness appeared, life kept its rhythm.

Cameryn's father, Patrick Mahoney, spoke again as his forehead furrowed into deep creases. "Well, you just tell the good sheriff he can wait for me to finish my breakfast. It's only seven in the morning, and a few more minutes won't make a whit of difference to the poor stiff in the tub. He's past caring." The person on the other end must have said something, because Patrick countered with, "I'm no ghoul, Deputy, I'm just the humble coroner. And just so you know, it's always better to eat before a call—the taste of decay stays in the mouth too long after. Good-bye." The phone clicked softly in its cradle and he looked up innocently, although Cameryn noticed his eyes twinkling.

"You shouldn't be tormenting the new deputy, son," Mammaw admonished in her soft Irish lilt. "You'll scare him away, is what you'll do. Not everyone can dance with the dead."

"Ah, the boy needs to toughen up," Patrick answered. "And I guess I'm a bit bent out of shape because the good sheriff was able to hire help while I've been left to carry the investigative load by myself."

"That's not the new deputy's fault. Don't be taking your frustrations out on him."

Patrick looked up from beneath shaggy brows. "Let's just say I've got other issues with Deputy Crowley. But enough about him—I want to enjoy what's left of my morning."

"You're right," Mammaw agreed, nodding. "Get the coffee going, girl!"

Cameryn, who'd already begun, pressed the button on the coffee grinder, then pulled the lid off and tapped the pulverized beans into a mound that looked like rich earth. It smelled good, too, dark and pungent.

"Make it extra strong, Cammie," her father instructed as he picked up the newspaper and snapped it open. "A floater first thing in the morning is a hard way to begin."

Cameryn moved on automatic pilot as she went through the motions of her one domestic skill. Her mind, though, worked the scene that her father would process in less than an hour. From her books she knew what happened to bodies left in water; mentally, she ticked off the steps her father would need to take as he took possession of the dead man. A cotton sheet, vinyl body bag, the digital camera, as well as the biohazard bags to contain any medication left in the room—all had to be loaded into the back of their old station wagon, the ancient car that doubled as the town hearse. Except for the camera, most of those items were stacked neatly on metal shelves in their garage along with the wheeled gurney and the box of latex gloves, ready to be pulled at a moment's notice.

She turned just in time to notice Mammaw crack a shell with one hand, empty its contents into a glass bowl, and toss it into the sink. It rattled into the hole of the garbage disposal like a ball in a net.

"Good shot," Cameryn said with a laugh. "Did you play ball in Ireland?"

"In my day girls didn't want to sweat—we were taught to take care of our families. Which reminds me—are you ready to learn how to properly crack an egg?"

Picturing the last time she'd tried to spread the shell single-handed and the mess she'd made, Cameryn shook her head no. Besides, she had bigger dreams than baking Pork in Guinness or Dublin Coddle—dreams of which her grandmother did not approve.

"Well? How about it, girl?" Mammaw pressed. "You're almost eighteen. It's time."

Cameryn looked at the eggs and wrinkled her nose. "You know I hate to cook."

"That's because you've never tried."

"No, that's because there are more interesting things to do."

Her grandmother looked at her sharply. "Like cutting into dead bodies?"

Cameryn swallowed back her irritation. "Yeah—the live ones kick too much."

"So now it's humor, is it? You don't fool me, not for a

minute," Mammaw said, pointing at her with a dripping shell. "Go ahead and make your jokes, but I'm worried about you. Your soul's getting dark lately. Don't think I haven't noticed. Why, in church last Sunday your lips barely moved when the creed was read. There was a time when you said the words louder than anybody. Now you just sit, your mind engrossed in God knows what."

Cameryn yanked open the silverware drawer and pulled out a knife and fork. Standing by her father, she set the silverware on the table harder than she needed to. "My soul is fine," she said.

"How can it be? Look at the ideas you take in. All those books you read on death and dying—blood spatter, bugs crawling over those poor devils. Oh yes, I've seen them." Her grandmother made a *tsk*ing sound behind her teeth. "All along I told my Pat that he's made a mistake encouraging you the way he does, but no one listens to me."

"Ma, don't start," he moaned from behind the *Silverton News*.

"Start what? I'm having a conversation with my only grandchild in my own kitchen."

Patrick snapped the paper even wider and buried himself behind its pages. *Thanks for the help, Dad,* Cameryn thought.

Her grandmother had wrapped herself in a new cotton robe. As usual, the sleeves were too long, and the bottom inch dragged across the kitchen floor like a terry mop.

The too-big garment made her look almost childlike, although Cameryn knew that her grandmother was anything but when it came to the subject of her granddaughter's future career. Mammaw hated forensics. Like a chicken pecking grain, her grandmother picked and nibbled at Cameryn's dream, convinced as she was that it would somehow twist Cameryn's soul.

"All I'm asking is this: Why can't you set your sights on becoming a *real* doctor?"

"A forensic pathologist *is* a real doctor." The irritation welled in her throat, and she could no longer swallow it.

"I mean a doctor who treats the living! With that brain of yours there are lots of things that you could do. You're a headstrong girl, Cammie, but that stubbornness can take you down the wrong path."

The heat rose inside her as she countered, "I've told you a hundred times that this is the path I want."

"Don't give me your cheek! It's that streak from your mother that's coming out, and that's the streak that'll get you in trouble!"

"For Pete's sake, Ma," her father cried, "leave her be!" He slapped the newspaper onto the table loud enough to make Cameryn jump. Suddenly he looked weary. "All I want to do is start my day in relative peace. I don't need the sound of my mother and my daughter ringing in my ears when I leave. Give a man a break!"

Chastened, Mammaw lifted her whisk and began to

beat the eggs so hard they turned to lemony foam in a matter of seconds. "I'm only speaking my mind," she muttered straight into the bowl. "I only want what's best for the girl."

For a moment there was no sound in the kitchen except her grandmother's whisk flicking in percussive rhythm. Cameryn stood, unsure of what to do while her grandmother's pale face turned to stone. She wanted to—what? Not run away exactly, but to be left alone. It almost made her laugh when she heard others complain about their parents, especially their mothers. Mammaw was not only from another country but, for all intents and purposes, another century.

Her father sighed, then carefully folded his paper and smoothed it between his fingers. Finally, he said, "Cameryn, honey, why don't you go outside and get me my folder, the one with the death certificates in it—you'll find it in the front seat, passenger side. Will you do that for me?"

"Sure," she said, relieved to be set free.

He grasped her hand as she went by and squeezed it gently. "And, um, take your time, okay?"

"Not a problem." The screen door squealed as she stepped outside into the cool morning air. The voices of her dad and grandmother rose and fell behind her, like swells on the sea. ". . . I'm doing the best I can, Ma. . . ."

"But son, I love that girl, and someone's got to pull her

from the shadows. . . . " They were fussing again. About her. She hated it when they did that.

Walking quickly, Cameryn passed rows of flowerpots her grandmother had planted at the first sign of spring. Now it was early October, which meant soon the plants would be brought into the warmth of their home to cheat death. Flowers and food—that's what her grandmother was about. Cameryn and her father got along well enough, but her grandmother was something else entirely. They were opposites bound by blood.

The difference began in the way they looked. Both her grandmother and her father were pure Mahoney through and through. Patrick stood as tall as a grizzly, with a broad, barrel chest and pawlike fists that waved through the air whenever he talked. Although his hair had faded, it had once been a fiery red, and his heavy brows seemed to grow out farther every passing year. Her grandmother was a smaller version, with the same blunt nose and ice-blue eyes, the same jaw that squared when she was worked up over something, which seemed to Cameryn to be too much of the time.

Cameryn, on the other hand, was much more diminutive, which made her look as different as she felt—small and thin-boned, with long, curly black hair that reached all the way to her waist. Her hair and her brown eyes were a gift from her maternal side, as were the high cheekbones and golden skin passed down from a distant

Cherokee relative. At least, that's what she'd been told. She had almost no memory at all of her mother, whom her father rarely spoke of. When Mammaw did, it was only as a warning. "Don't be doing that," she'd say. "It's what *she* used to do," or, "No, girl, that's what *she* thought."

It would be easier, Cameryn knew, if her mother were dead. There would have been some finality in that. Instead, her mother had just disappeared one day, and after that, there were a few letters, and then . . . nothing. Hannah Mahoney was a stranger who hadn't bothered to call or write in years, a ghost who never haunted. Once, when Cameryn was six, she and her father had curled up on their swing, watching the twilight deepen to the velvet of night until the stars appeared, first pale, and then bright as they burned into the night sky.

"Tell me about Mommy," she'd asked.

Against the rhythm of the squeaking swing he told her about Hannah, how she had loved dogs and the color blue and other things Cameryn could no longer remember. But she still could recall snuggling into her father's scratchy wool jacket and asking, "But why did she go? Where is she?"

"I—I don't know. I just don't know," he'd whispered into her hair. "But I have to believe that one day soon she'll come to us. She'll get better and she'll come home. You'll see."

As the years passed he spoke of her less and less, until he stopped mentioning Hannah's name altogether. There'd been no divorce, no explanation, nothing. Sometimes, in the quiet of the night, she would allow herself to think of her mother, but only for a moment. It was better to focus on the practical, on the here and now, on things she could taste and see and touch. Her reality was the Mahoney Trinity—mother, son, and granddaughter— all living in the green-shingled house high in the San Juan Mountains in a town no bigger than a Post-it note.

Cameryn retrieved the folder from the front seat of the station wagon and returned to the kitchen, waiting long enough to be sure they weren't still talking about her. They weren't. It was quiet inside, except for the chopping sound of her mammaw's knife on the wooden board and her father's gentle slurping of coffee. While they went on with their morning, Cameryn let the plan form in her mind, the one she'd thought about before but that was now taking shape, a piece at a time. Just this morning the final piece had slipped into place. Exhaling a deep breath, she walked to the table and set down the folder.

"Thanks, Cam," he said, without looking up. "Just wanted to be sure I wasn't out of certificates." He peered into the envelope and said, "Good. I've got two left."

Cameryn took the coffeepot to the table and refilled her father's mug. "What's going to happen to the body when you're done with it?"

"Oh, most likely a pauper's grave. The sheriff thinks the man's a transient so his body'll probably end up unclaimed, with no one caring what time he died or that he died at all. You know," he said, suddenly thoughtful, "it's a sad world we live in when a human being leaves so little of a mark that no one even realizes it when he's gone."

Cameryn heard a snap as her mammaw pushed the button on the toaster. "You reap what you sow," she said. "Now let's talk about something more pleasant, like the weather, for instance. If you'd look out the window you'd see it's like summer outside, warmer than it's been this time of year for as long as I can remember. Here, girl, take this!" Her grandmother reached out the plate, loaded with food, and Cameryn took it and set it in front of Pat on the yellow gingham place mat. Yellow was her grandmother's favorite color, one she wove through the room like a golden thread. "I like my kitchen cheerful," she'd say, "because the kitchen is the soul of the house." True to her word, the round oak table always had fresh yellow flowers in the middle, the blooms nodding lazily in the sun like sleepy heads.

Now Cameryn stole a glance at her grandmother, who had at this point turned her attention to running water into a pot.

"What is it, Cammie?" Patrick asked.

Startled, Cameryn could only look at him blankly.

Patrick focused his gaze on her with sudden intensity. "You've got a strange look on your face and you're chewing your nails again. I know you," he said, wagging a piece of toast at her, "you're up to something. What's in your head?"

Cameryn pulled her fingers away from her mouth, a habit that betrayed her when she was nervous. Shrugging, she smiled and said, "Nothing."

"Come on, now, it's not like you to play games."

She shot a quick glance at her grandmother, who was now engrossed in her scrubbing. Her father leaned toward her and she lowered her voice to just above a whisper. "All right. I have this idea. Actually, I've had it for a long time, but—that doesn't matter. Anyway, what I'm going to say is going to sound crazy but I want you to hear all of it before you say no."

He munched his toast. "How about I just say no now and save the time."

"Come on, Dad! Listen, the sheriff got an assistant to help him when *you're* the one who could use a hand. You always say you've got too much to do and not enough time to do it in. You need your own assistant."

He whispered now, too, leaning in conspiratorially. "Right. Except there's a problem: There's not a lot of coroner material in Silverton."

"But I know a person. I'm thinking of someone who'd be ready to go at a moment's notice," she went on eagerly.

"Somebody who understands the field. Someone you could trust."

"And just who is the miracle worker of Silverton?"

Cameryn paused for just a moment. Glancing over to make sure Mammaw wasn't listening, she whispered, "Me."

"You!"

"Yes, me. Let me work for you."

Her father pulled back in order to stare at her full in the face, his blue eyes squinting at her as though he'd never seen her before. Forgetting to keep his voice low, he said, "Oh, baby, you don't know what you're asking. It's a hard job—different from what you see in your books. What I do is real life. We're just a tiny operation, which means I do it all. I'm the one who has to pull dead people out of cars and lift waterlogged corpses out of bathtubs. You don't want to see that. Besides, your grandmother's worried enough about you as it is. . . ."

Cameryn knew this would be his first line of objection, but her mind had already worked it through and she was ready with her defense. "But there's nothing to worry about. I'm a straight-A student. I don't do drugs or smoke or do any of that stuff. And I already know what I want to do with my life: I want to go into forensics. You're always saying we don't get enough time together and this would change that. Dad, my plan makes sense—you know it does."

"Except you're too young to be sure that this is your future," he countered. "Why don't we wait and see if that's what you want later, like, say, when you're out of college?"

"So you're penalizing me because I already know what I want."

"No, no, no," he said, his brow furrowed with concentration. "I'm saying seventeen is still young, Cammie. Death is a hard business. Why subject yourself to it?"

She stood, silent, because there was no way to answer. Since she was a science geek she was of course drawn to its absolutes, and those would be her tools in forensics. What happened when a person died and the puzzle of death was part of it, too. But it was more than that. In her books she saw bodies in every conceivable level of decay, some felled by their own biology while others had been taken at the hands of a killer, and yet the dead all had one, tragic thing in common: They had no voice. At times she wondered at the parallel between herself, her past, and the dead she wanted to serve. It was a strange thought, really, because she had a perfectly good home with loving people watching over her. And yet . . . a whole section of her life had been buried along with Hannah's memory. How did that make her feel? In a way she felt silenced, too. It was the power to give voice that had drawn her to forensics. The dead told a story that the pathologist, if she were good enough, could hear, and Cameryn wanted to be that person. She wanted to be the translator. And maybe, when she learned that language, she could in turn speak for herself. But all of that was too complicated for the morning's question. When pressed by her father again, she just shrugged. "I don't know," she said. "I just want to. And I want to start learning now."

"Absolutely not!" her grandmother roared from her station behind the sink. Cameryn's head jerked up in time to see the pot clatter into the porcelain sink. Her grandmother's hands were planted firmly on her hips and she looked taller, Cameryn realized, than she had just moments before.

"Patrick, tell her no!" Mammaw's finger pointed at Cameryn. "And shame on you for even asking such a thing! It's out of the question!"

Her father leaned back in his chair so that it balanced on just two legs. He seemed to stare at his half-eaten eggs as though he could divine the answer from them, as though they were entrails read by the prophets of old. Something was going on in his mind, and that something gave Cameryn hope. He hadn't said no yet. In fact, he didn't say anything.

"Come on, Dad," she whispered. "Please."

"You can't be considering this—Patrick, it's taking her down the wrong path. Are you listening to me? She needs to stay away from darkness. You know what I'm saying. Are you listening to me?"

Slowly, Patrick's chair tipped forward until it came to

rest with a thump on the wooden floor. "I'm listening," he answered quietly. "And I don't like what I'm hearing."

"You can't mean that!"

"Ma, you and me, we're both too afraid. How many years has it been?" He shook his head wearily. "We're running around, chasing ghosts, and we've got to stop."

"You're making a mistake!" Mammaw cried, but Patrick didn't seem to hear.

"We've got to stop," he said again. "We've got to let Cameryn decide who she wants to be." Her grandmother stood frozen, waiting, while Cameryn felt her own blood thaw as her heart beat again. Finally, her father slapped his knee and said, "All right then."

"All *right*?" Cameryn asked, elated.

"Yes. All right," he told her. "Cameryn, you're officially hired as assistant to the coroner of Silverton, Colorado. How does ten dollars an hour sound?"

"I love you, Dad!" she cried, sliding onto her father's lap. His strong arms encircled her, pulling her tight. She could hear the gurgle of his stomach beneath his shirt. She heard something else, too: her grandmother's slippered feet as they stomped across the floor and the slam of the door as she left the kitchen.

"How mad is she?" she asked in a small voice.

"She'll get over it—Cammie, she's a good woman. She's tried to be your mother, to do what's best for you. She's worried you'll go too far into the macabre." With his finger he pulled up her chin, and his blue eyes looked worried. "You won't, will you?"

"No." She returned his gaze, unflinching. "I just like the science."

"I like the way the dead don't talk back. Makes for a lot less friction on the job."

"Oh, but they do. They still tell us their stories."

"You're right. I guess I just never thought of it that way." He slid her from his lap and stood, picking up his folder with the two death certificates inside. "We'd better move. There's a dead man waiting for us," he said. "Let's go find out what he has to say."

Chapter Two

"WE'RE GOING TO NEED a tarp, just in case," her father said, flipping down the backseat of their station wagon to make room for the body they'd be picking up. His voice sounded muffled as he added, "We'll need a sheet, too. And heavy gloves. The guy's skin might have come off in the water and we'll have to fish it out of the drain, which is a job you'll want the long gloves for. You okay?"

"Sure. I already told you, I can handle it!" Cameryn answered with more confidence than she felt. When her father's head reemerged from the car, she asked, "What do you want me to do?"

"Smooth this down in the back." He tossed her a heavy tarp. "It's an added protection against body fluid leakage, although if we do our job right none should seep out of

the bag. I'll get the gurney and then we're out of here."
Patrick's feet crunched on gravel as he disappeared into
the Mahoney garage, a small one-car affair crammed to
the gills with boxes and storage shelves. There was barely enough room for Mammaw's gold Oldsmobile in the
center of the garage; from the outside looking in, the car
looked like a giant pig-in-a-blanket. Both Cameryn, who
had a 1987 Jeep Cherokee, and her father, who owned the
station wagon, were forced to park outside year-round—
fine in the summer but hard in winter. Some mornings it
took Cameryn half an hour to scrape away the heavy
mountain snow that settled on her windshield like a
thick shroud, a common occurrence at ten thousand feet.

Cameryn crawled into the back of their station wagon
and patted down the plastic sheet. Her father reemerged
with a gurney.

"Your wheel's got a squeak," she told him, hopping out
to join him.

"Yeah, but my customers haven't complained yet." With
one smooth motion, her father collapsed the gurney flat
and slid it and the body bag into the car's bay. The hatch
slammed shut with a resounding thud. "Okay," he said.
"It's showtime."

It was Patrick Mahoney's job, Cameryn knew, to pro-
nounce the Silverton residents formally and legally
deceased. Most of those who died were sent on to funeral
homes, but if he had any doubt at all concerning the cause

of death, her father would order an autopsy, which would be performed in Durango, the closest place with a forensic lab. That also meant transporting the body in their family station wagon. Many a corpse made its final trip in the back of the car the Mahoneys did their grocery shopping in, a fact that seemed to trouble Cameryn's friends. Her best friend, Lyric, was so convinced she'd seen a ghost's pale face pressed into the station wagon's rear window that she'd vowed to never ride in their car again.

"But why," Cameryn had asked Lyric, "would a ghost haunt our station wagon? Why would it waste a perfectly good afterlife tooling around Silverton in that old beater?" Lyric never answered, but she never got in the car again, either.

Now, as her father pulled out of the Mahoney driveway, Cameryn tried to quell the nerves fluttering inside. "Do you think you'll need to order an autopsy on this floater-guy?" she asked.

Her father sighed as he shifted the station wagon into forward. "Possibly. I sure hope he turns out to be a natural. Makes my job a heck of a lot easier."

"A 'natural'?"

"Oh, so you don't know everything about this business just yet?" he said with a sly smile. "That's good. It means I can still teach you a thing or two. Calling a person a 'natural' is a bit of coroner shorthand—means the person died from natural causes."

"How can you tell if they're a 'natural' if the body's not autopsied?"

"Well, there are protocols I follow. If it's an attended death or if there's a known medical condition, well, that would explain why the person died. If that's the case, they're considered a natural and my job is done. Remember the time you found me in the rest home when I was processing that old lady?" He glanced at her and said, "She was a classic natural, so no autopsy."

Cameryn nodded. She'd found him in the room of an elderly woman, his head bent in concentration as he filled out forms only two feet from the corpse. She remembered drifting over to the woman's bed, not afraid, but curious to look at death up close. The woman's skin and hair were as white as parchment; blue-veined hands rested lightly on the blanket's edge, her yellowed fingernails touching as if in prayer. It was the woman's eyes, though, that Cameryn remembered most. Still open, they stared at the ceiling with an expression that was serene but vacant, as though she were nothing more than an empty husk with its insides removed.

"So that old lady died from pneumonia," her father went on, flipping on his blinker. "She'd been under a doctor's care, so I released her and she was sent straight on to the funeral home. With any luck this guy'll have some sort of condition and we'll be able to skip the autopsy, which can get pretty dicey when it's a decomp. Otherwise"—he made a cutting motion with his hands—"we're going in."

They turned onto Greene Street and headed west. Cameryn knew it wouldn't take long to travel the entire length of the town, since Silverton was home to only seven hundred people. A tiny, inbred community, her town was populated with an odd mix of working men and women, leather-skinned ranchers, and upscale shop owners who wedged American flags into their flower boxes like patriotic quills.

By all rights Silverton should have died years ago like so many other mining towns scattered throughout the West, but against the odds it had clung to life. When Silverton's gold, silver, and copper veins finally played out, the miners who worked them were forced to leave camps that had existed for over eighty years. But the miners' free-flowing money had been Silverton's lifeblood, and without their cash, the bars and gambling halls began to close their doors. Desperate, the mayor convinced the Durango & Silverton Narrow Gauge Railroad to haul a more lucrative payload to the town: passengers.

It was then that Silverton reinvented itself as a haven for tourists. With the stroke of a politician's pen, the town became a mandatory two-hour stop at the end of the D & S tracks. Cameryn's grandmother remembered what it had been like in Silverton before its transformation into respectability. "In the old days we had a red-light district on Blair Street, with many a bordello and speakeasy. Mind you, it was a place of terrible sin," she'd said. "But I remember the flavor of it. Oh, I'm glad it's gone, but we've lost something, girl."

Now Silverton's Greene Street was studded with quaint shops, hotels, and old-fashioned eateries. The new, improved Silverton looked as polished as its name—clean and scrubbed bright as a lighted Christmas village.

Patrick turned south, away from the born-again buildings, and then made a quick right onto Copper Street and a moment later he stopped in front of a run-down motel built in the shape of an *L*. A hand-painted sign declaring CHILDREN SLEEP FREE tipped drunkenly from the motel roof, while the parking lot, paved only in gravel, boasted a mere two cars. One room at the end of the long side of the *L* was decked with yellow plastic tape emblazoned with the words DO NOT CROSS. A slender young man, looking barely older than Cameryn, paced just beyond the tape. His dark hair was almost too long to be an officer's, curling gently as it did over his collar. He wore a pair of jeans instead of khakis, although his shirt was regulation. A small badge on his breast pocket glinted in the light. He seemed to be waiting for them.

"There's that fool deputy," her father said. His voice came out in a growl.

"Why don't you like him?" Cameryn asked.

Patrick's eyes narrowed as he ran his hand along the back of his neck. "Let's just say he pokes his nose into things he shouldn't and then tries to make like he's doing you a favor. Stay away from that one, Cammie."

She glanced back at the deputy, who by now had stopped pacing. He stood with his boots firmly planted to the ground, his fists shoved into his jeans pockets, his shoulders squared. When he saw they were looking at him, he pulled one hand free in a halfhearted wave, then returned to pacing.

"All right, let's get back to business," Patrick said. "First thing you do is write down when we arrive." He put his hand on her arm. "What time is it?"

Cameryn looked at her watch. "It's seven thirty-seven. I marked down seven thirty as my starting point since that's when we left the house, which means I've already made"—she did some swift mental calculations—"almost a dollar twenty-five without lifting a finger. I knew I'd like this job!"

"Ah, there's my girl, always ready to put the screws to the establishment. And what is that I see in your hand? Is that Vicks?"

"Uh-huh." She held up the small blue cylinder, proud that she'd thought to bring it, and said, "I'm going to smear some under my nose, you know, in case there's a bad smell."

"Good planning, but here's the thing. Using Vicks will open up your sinuses, which actually lets in more of the odor."

"Really?" Cameryn could feel herself wilt. She'd managed to make a mistake without even getting out of the car.

"It's a rookie error. You don't want to inhale more of the guy, do you?" He reached behind the seat and retrieved a plastic bag. "Use peppermint oil. And put on these gloves. We'll save the heavy ones to use if the need arises." Handing her a small vial of the oil and a pair of thin latex gloves—the kind doctors used—he said, "Don't forget the camera."

"Not a problem."

Grunting, he slid himself out and slammed the car door behind him. While her father went to the back of the station wagon, Cameryn pulled down the visor and opened the clip-on mirror. She carefully smeared her upper lip with the oil, which smelled good but burned her skin, then pulled the gloves on, wiggling her fingers into the ends and snapping the wristbands as she stepped out of the car. She felt official. Ready. But her father stood in front of the door, waving his hands at Deputy Crowley, who had blocked his entrance. Cameryn rushed to join them.

"This is important. Just give me a chance to explain!"

Her father's voice was curt. "Let me pass, Deputy."

She was closer now, and she couldn't help but notice that Crowley was good-looking—she had to admit that. His eyebrows and lashes were darker than his hair, which had the effect of making his eyes seem electric. From where she stood it was hard to tell what color they were, either blue or green. From the deep tan of his skin she knew he spent a lot of time outdoors. Following her father's lead, she smoothed her features with what she hoped looked like cool disinterest as she stepped next to her father.

"But what I have to say is important, sir," Deputy Crowley pressed.

"Is it about the man in the tub?"

"No. It's about the other . . . matter." For the briefest instant his eyes flashed at Cameryn. *Green,* she decided.

"Not interested," her father snapped. Waving his hand dismissively, he said, "If you want to make yourself useful, go get the manager and bring him back to the room so I can talk to him personally." He began to walk away.

"Sheriff Jacobs already talked to him."

"I want to talk to him myself. And get the gurney and body bag out of the back of the station wagon and bring them inside. Lock my car when you're done." Turning, he tossed the car keys, which Crowley caught in midair. "Come on, Cammie. We've got work to do."

She could feel the deputy's eyes on her back as she ducked under the police tape, but the closer she got to the room the easier it was to push him from her mind. Ahead of her was her very first forensic case. She'd read theory after theory in her books, but this was reality and the difference made her almost dizzy. A puzzle etched in the remains of a human, ready for her to decipher, and she felt her hands begin to sweat inside the gloves.

The first thing she noticed inside was the odor, faint over the peppermint but still there. It was sickly-sweet, like rotten meat doused in cologne, and her stomach clamped hard against it. She took a quick series of breaths, quickly switching to inhaling through her mouth instead of her nose. In front of her was a short, narrow hallway, then, to the left, the room itself.

Patrick placed his hand on her shoulder and squeezed hard. "It's a bit ripe in here."

"Do you ever get used to it?"

He shook his head. "The stench always makes you want to toss your cookies. Occupational hazard."

She tried not to notice the flies that buzzed through the air in tiny squadrons. Dozens walked along a closed door directly on her left, which she supposed was the bathroom, the place where the body lay. Straight ahead was a window, and to the left of that was the motel room itself. As she entered she saw Sheriff John Jacobs by the bed, scratching notes on a small spiral notebook he held in his hand. She hadn't seen him from the hallway.

"Morning, Pat," he said, nodding. "Oh, hello there, Cameryn." His eyebrows shot up as he dipped his head, staring at her over his glasses. "What in the Sam Hill are you doing here?"

"I'm working with my dad now," she replied, still breathing through her mouth. "I'm his new assistant."

"Assistant? Really? Is that so?" The sheriff looked at her father skeptically. He was a short man, with gray, thinning hair, along with sharp features and a thin nose. Jacobs's mouth twitched as he asked, "You think that's a good idea, Pat? The man's been in there awhile. It'll be pretty rough on the girl."

Patrick crossed his arms over his ample chest and leaned back on his heels. That was his stubborn stance, Cameryn thought, grinning to herself. Jacobs didn't have a chance. "My Cammie's got a mind to go into forensics and she wants to see what's what. She's not like other girls—she's twice as smart as most and half as squeamish as the rest."

"Yeah, well, take a look at the guy before you decide," Jacobs countered.

Without another word, Patrick walked to the bathroom. Cameryn heard the flies buzzing angrily as he yanked the door open and then, for a moment, all was still. Since Jacobs was pretending to read his notepad, Cameryn studied the pale, ghostly square on the wall where a picture must have been removed and waited for the verdict. When her father emerged from the bathroom, a wave of air, thick with stench, rolled into Cameryn's mouth, and suddenly she could taste the man. She stifled her instinct to cover her face with her hands.

"Okay, I admit it, he's pretty far gone." Patrick didn't meet her gaze when he said this, which told her all that she needed to know. Her father had changed his mind—her pass into the coroner's secret world had been rescinded.

"Dad, don't!" she protested. "I can do this."

"You can help me process the room itself," he answered with false cheer.

Jacobs scratched at the skin behind his ear. "Speaking of which, who's paying her salary? I don't remember voting on this. You can't just up and hire somebody without it getting approved."

"Cameryn's wages are coming out of my own pocket, which is more than I can say for that deputy of yours. The good citizens of Silverton are footing the bill for him, and I, for one, want my money back."

"All right, all right," Jacobs answered. "No need to get testy. I was just asking."

"So, John," Patrick asked, "what have you got?"

It was clear the two of them had shut her out. Cameryn felt as though she were standing behind a piece of glass she couldn't walk through. Hadn't her father just said she was twice as smart as most girls? Hadn't he said she could be his partner? None of that seemed to matter now. Frustrated, she hugged the wall and watched as Jacobs flipped the pages in his notebook.

"Let's get this thing done," he said. "The wife's got cinnamon rolls waiting." He cleared his throat. As the sheriff began to read, his voice became dispassionate, as though he were reciting names from a phone book. "The manager opened the door about an hour ago 'cause Robertson—first name Larry—was supposed to check out yesterday and didn't. Rullon said he followed his nose to the bathroom there." Jacobs paused to point the end of his pen toward the hallway.

"Who's Rullon?" Cameryn broke in. If they wouldn't let her see the body she could still get in the game.

The sheriff gave her a look. "Rullon Sage. The manager. You know that old-timer who runs around wearing red suspenders? He's the real skinny guy. Smokes a pipe."

"Oh, yeah, I know him," she said, nodding. "He comes into the Grand sometimes. He's a lousy tipper."

Jacobs gave her another look. "So, back to what I was saying. Rullon told me he poked his head inside the room and gave a holler, but no one answered. He opened the bathroom door. He said he hurried right back to his office and called us 'cause it was clear Larry didn't need no doctor."

"I'm sure the smell told him that," Patrick said. "I don't know if Rullon's ever going to be able to use that tub again."

"If it was me I'd rip the whole thing out and chuck it," Jacobs agreed.

The room was littered with old clothing and cigarette butts; three empty whiskey bottles lay scattered across the floor like bowling pins. As the men talked, Cameryn went over to the bed, which was crumpled and unmade. There was a smell here, too, but this one was of cigarettes mingled with stale urine. A thin layer of grime seemed to have settled over everything, dulling the surfaces with a gray film. Even the window seemed opaque.

"I asked Rullon when was the last time he'd seen the guy," Jacobs was saying, "and he said four days ago—the day the man checked in." His reading glasses had slipped down his nose, and he pushed them up with his index finger. "Four days is a mighty big window, Pat. It's gonna be a challenge fixing time of death, let alone cause."

"Yeah, and from the looks of it I'm guessing he's a drinker. But a bunch of empty whiskey bottles won't tell enough of the story." Sighing deeply, her father said, "We may be in for an autopsy."

Cameryn's gaze went back to the bed. The cheap polyester cover had been pulled down halfway, and the pillow had a depression in its middle. Only one side of the bed was unmade, though—the other side was as smoothed and tucked as an unopened letter. For some reason the empty half of the bed made her feel a bit sad. Had loneliness driven this man to alcohol? What kind of life must he have had to end up rotting in a cheap motel? But then again, what good did it do to wonder about the reasons?

she chided herself. People made choices and people died. It was her job to figure out the death, not the life.

Her father and the sheriff were deep in a different conversation, this time about the budget and how Silverton would have to foot the bill for the autopsy. Once again she looked around. An old gym bag had been tossed on the floor. Squatting, she searched through it but found nothing save some dirt that had settled into the seams. Next, she turned her attention to a small lamp on the nightstand next to the bed. The bulb had been left on. Beneath the light she found a plastic cup, half-filled with water, which had been placed next to a pad of paper and an ashtray overflowing with the remains of crumpled cigarettes. In writing so wobbly she could barely decipher it, Cameryn made out the beginnings of what she guessed to be a phone number. It began with a string of numbers, but then the wobbly line faded out in a shepherd's crook, the last digit incomplete.

She put her hand onto the pad; even through her plastic glove the paper felt warm to the touch. That meant the light must have been on a long time—maybe days—even when the room had been lit by natural sunlight. Curious, she opened the nightstand drawer and searched inside. There was nothing in there except a tattered phone book and an open book of matches. On a hunch she pulled out the phone book—hadn't he been writing down a number?—with the idea of checking the partial number to a liquor store. As if on cue the pages fell open in her hand to a place where a small baggie had been inserted between its leaves. "Hell-o," she murmured to herself. When she held the crumpled baggie to the light she saw a dozen yellow hexagons, stamped with the number 80. There was a prescription inside the bag as well, dirty and dog-eared.

"Hey, what you got there, Cammie?" her father asked.

At the sound of her name, Cameryn felt her scalp jump. "Uh—I was just—I saw a partial number written on this pad here and I thought maybe our guy was going through the phone book before he died. I found this baggie inside. It's okay that I picked it up, right?"

"As long as you've got your gloves on. Like I told you, the coroner owns the effects of the deceased. The sheriff can't touch anything," he said, raising his eyebrows, "but we can."

"So what's in the bag, Cameryn?" Jacobs asked.

"There's some loose pills and a prescription for . . . I think it says . . . 'Inderal.'" She smoothed the baggie between her fingers and read the scrolling print. "Yeah, it's Inderal. It was prescribed to Lawrence Robertson. Wait, I think there's more than one prescription inside." She opened the bag and fanned three prescriptions in her hands like playing cards. "Looks like there's one a month for three more months, all for Inderal."

Sheriff Jacobs pulled the end of his long nose. "Inderal? What the heck is that?"

Her father seemed pleased. Walking over to Cameryn, he took the baggie from her hand. "It's a drug used for esophageal varices."

"Tell me in English," Sheriff Jacobs snapped.

"It's for enlarged veins in the esophagus. If they open up a person can bleed to death." Squinting, Patrick held the baggie closer to the light. "Looks like Doc Kearney down in Durango wrote it for the deceased. Inderal's a pill that's prescribed when a patient's a boozehound. I'd bet our Mr. Robertson had some serious liver damage to go along with the varices. So he was drinking while taking Inderal. Mmm, mmm, mmm, Cameryn may have found our answer. Nice work. Don't know if I would have thought to look there."

Cameryn flushed with the compliment. It felt good to work with her father, as a team and almost as equals.

"So what's next?" Jacobs asked.

"I'll call the doc and see what he has to say. If he tells me Robertson was on his last legs we'll just skip the autopsy and call it a day." Then, to Cameryn, he asked, "By the way, where's the camera?"

Cameryn felt her eyes widen as she realized her mistake. Her job was to photograph the scene and she'd already forgotten her camera and disturbed the evidence. Was the case ruined? "I'm—I'm sorry, Dad," she said. "I left it in the car."

"Oh, for heaven's sake, don't look so panicked. This isn't

a homicide. Just go get it now and start shooting the bed and the drawer and all of that. And next time, pictures before you move things, okay?"

"Sure," she said, nodding. "Absolutely."

Sheriff Jacobs ambled over to Pat, who pulled at the next flimsy drawer, checking for more clues. Cameryn made her way to the hallway and was about to leave when she found herself stopping at the bathroom door. The flies had ceased their buzzing but not their crawling, which created a strange pattern, like a kaleidoscope of undulating black. She could not be seen from where she stood, and that fact gave her pause. The doorknob, dirty brass with a dent in its middle, seemed to stare at her like a single eye.

Well, why not? she asked herself fiercely. Why shouldn't she? She wanted to see the man who had slept in only half his bed and washed down pills with whiskey. She wanted to see a real case and apply her book knowledge, and there was no doubt she could handle the gruesome sight. The two men were patronizing her. As quickly as that, she settled it in her mind: She was going in. As she inched closer to the bathroom door, the flies sensed her. They launched from the door, encircling her head, landing in her hair. Batting them away, she turned the knob. When she pushed the bathroom door open, the drone of flies grew louder, and then, in earnest, she fought the urge to turn and run.

In front of her an arm stretched out from the tub like a tree branch ending in gnarled fingers. The nails were dirty and thick, more like chips of wood than fingertips. A hundred flies or more walked delicately along the flesh of the exposed limb. The body looked bloated and grotesque, more surreal than human. Holding her breath, she moved until she could see his upper torso still propped in a seated position. His neck rested against the edge of the tub and his chin dropped open so that his bottom teeth showed. The eyes were open and sunken; more flies crawled over the vacant pupils that stared like bits of dusty glass. Robertson was a grizzled old man, pale and cold and unceremoniously dead, a man with dirty fingernails and underwater skin stretched so taut it looked like wax.

Still holding her breath, she moved closer, repelled and drawn at the same time. Something on the man's face was moving. His skin? He was dead and yet alive, and her mind connected sideways—movement equaled life. For an instant she could make no sense of her own perception. Leaning closer, she tried to understand, then jerked back in horror as she realized the source.

The movement was from maggots. Tiny larvae wiggled out from beneath his eyelids like grains of crackling rice. They slid from his nose and in his mouth along his tongue, moved from the canals of his ears to migrate down his neck. Frozen, Cameryn stood transfixed until she suddenly realized her urgent need for air. With her hands over her mouth and nose she took a deep, gulping breath. Her peppermint oil, her finger, nothing could stem the sickly sweet scent of rotting flesh that filled her nose, her mouth, her very insides. She was breathing in particles of Larry Robertson. Her stomach twisted over on itself like a coil, and she knew then that she would throw up.

Gagging, she raced through the bathroom door and out of the motel room and away from the sight and smell of death. Her legs pumped hard as she sprinted around the back of the motel to where the trash cans were propped. She leaned over until she was doubled in two; a second later she threw up into the garbage can, retching from the deepest part of her, glad her father wasn't watching, glad he hadn't seen her fail. She puked until she was dry, coughing so hard her eyes teared and her stomach ached. Even with her eyes closed she could still see the maggots and their flickering movements. She wiped her mouth with the back of her hand and stood, her hands trembling, her throat on fire.

Something touched her lightly on the shoulder. Whirling around, she stared straight into the eyes of Deputy Crowley.

Chapter Three

THROUGH THE BLUR SHE COULD see him, and she noticed with a start that his eyes were a strange color, neither green nor blue but somewhere in between, like the water in the high mountain lakes.

"Here," he told her, pressing tissues into her hand. "Take these. Nothing's as bad as the smell of death, except maybe maggots. I just about lost it when I saw him, too."

Cameryn took the fistful of Kleenex and wiped her mouth hard. What could be worse than to be caught puking her guts out, especially in front of a guy her father hated? Embarrassment shot through her as she realized some vomit had landed on her shirt, right on her breast pocket. She tried to wipe it, but only made the smear worse.

"I'd offer to help, but you might slap me," the deputy said. He smiled a slow smile.

Was he laughing at her? After all her talk of wanting to be a forensic pathologist, she was exposed now as the fraud she was. No doubt he'd tell everyone in town that Cameryn Mahoney couldn't take it. Balling up the tissue, she threw it into the garbage can with as much force as she could. "I gotta go," she told him. "My dad's waiting."

"Hey, Cameryn, don't look so mad. I just saw your pop—he was in the middle of telling Jacobs what a great job you did finding those pills in a phone book. He said he'd take you on every case from now on."

Cameryn just stood there, waiting. What was she supposed to say to that?

"He thinks you're a genius."

"A genius. Yeah, right. I really look smart right now, don't I?"

"There's nothing wrong with being human, Cameryn." He seemed to linger over every word, as though he had all the time in the world to talk to her. He leaned his elbow against the wall, propping up his lanky frame. "Your pop asked if I'd seen you. Don't worry, I covered for you."

She felt her heart jump sideways. "What did you say?"

"I said your cell phone went off and you were taking the call. That *was* a cell phone I saw in your back jeans pocket, wasn't it?"

Cameryn just stared at him. Had he been looking at her rear end?

"I make it a point to be observant," he said, his voice still slow and easy.

Raking her fingers through her hair, she pulled at the net of loose strands that had fallen into her face while bent over the garbage can. "So you lied," she said finally. "You lied to my dad."

A curl of a smile tugged at the corner of his mouth. "Only a little."

Deputy Crowley was as tall as her father but leaner, and when he moved his motions were smooth, as if his joints were well oiled. With his wide-set eyes and strong jaw he was easily handsome—the kind of good-looking that understood its own power. A small sliver of a scar stretched from his ear to his chin, made more noticeable against his tan, although his cheekbones and the tip of his nose had deepened to red. Cameryn hesitated. She knew she'd be in trouble if her father caught her talking to him—that much he'd made clear. And yet she knew her curiosity was even stronger than her sense of caution. What did her father have against this deputy? Glancing around quickly she saw the alley was empty, save for a gray cat walking daintily along the fence line. She turned back to him. "Do you have a first name, Deputy?"

"Justin."

"You're new here."

He nodded. "That's right. Which must be why I haven't run into you before now. But I do know a little about you.

I know you work at the Grand Hotel as a waitress."

Surprised, she asked, "Who told you that?"

The smile again. "I have my sources."

"I don't like it when people talk about me."

"Even when it's good?" He shifted more of his weight against the wall. "You know, I've been meaning to come by and grab lunch at the Grand. I'll try to come by next time you're on shift. I didn't know the girls in Silverton were so pretty or I'd have moved here years ago."

It was her turn to smile. Was he hitting on her? If he was, he was doing it badly, and yet his awkward play somehow emboldened her. She took a step in his direction, her arms crossed over her chest, hiding the stain, holding herself in. "First of all, I'm a server, not a waitress. Second, I'm a woman, not a girl. And third"—she leaned closer, her voice low—"my dad doesn't like you. He won't tell me why, but he's a smart man. If he doesn't like you"—she tilted her head up toward his—"I can't like you, either."

His voice was equally soft as he bent his head toward her until he was so near she could smell the peppermint on his breath. He was chewing gum; he snapped it between his teeth. "I bet your pop didn't tell you why he hates my guts, did he? Bet he clammed right up when it came to the details. Am I right?"

She could feel a flush creep into her scalp.

"You don't have to say anything, Cameryn. I can see the answer in your eyes."

"You can't see squat," she said, angry that he could read her so clearly. "My dad—he told me everything!"

"Now who's the liar?" He pulled away and straightened to his full height. "And I bet you'd like me to tell you all about it, but I won't. Not now, anyway. See, sometimes they kill the messenger." He winked and said, "You'd better get back and take your pictures before they notice you're gone. Don't want Daddy thinking you've been talking to the wrong people. See you around, Cammie."

"Wait—"

But Justin kept walking.

"How am I supposed to find out if you won't tell me?"

For a moment she thought he was going to turn the corner of the building without answering, but at the last second he stopped. Spinning on his heel, he faced her and gave her a slight bow. Then, with two fingers pressed to his forehead he sent her a mock salute. "You're the genius, Cameryn," he told her. "You figure it out."

"I heard the new deputy's really cute," Rachel announced to Cameryn. "I mean he's too old for you, but *I'm* almost nineteen and my sister told me the deputy's only twenty-one. Of course I'm leaving for college soon so there's not exactly much of a future, but I say why not at least try it out until I have to go? I don't think two years is too much of a difference in age. What do you know about him?"

Cameryn shook her head and continued wiping down

the table while Rachel Geller, her fellow server, chattered on as she always did. The smell of bleach burned Cameryn's eyes and nostrils. Her boss always soaked the cloths in a too-strong solution, but today it didn't bother her. After her stint with Robertson she had drenched her hands in her own bleach solution until her outer layer of skin seemed to dissolve, leaving her hands smooth and slick and sanitized. And yet, when she'd held her hands to her nose, she could still smell the lingering scent of the dead man. It seemed as if his very pores had fused into hers. "You'll get used to it," her father had assured her, but she wondered.

"I can't believe you saw some dead guy," Rachel went on. "It's already all over town. You are *so* not like me. If I had seen some rotting corpse in a bathtub I would have absolutely lost it. But nothing bothers you. You are, like, the toughest girl I know." She looked at Cameryn with frank admiration. "Sometimes I think you're more like a guy."

"What do you mean?" Cameryn asked, her voice sharp.

Rachel's blue eyes widened as she realized her mistake. "No, I didn't mean it *that* way. It's because you're into science and all that boy stuff. I'm not saying you're *like* a guy, it's just—you know you're not—never mind, I'm only making it worse." A redhead, Rachel had dyed her hair chestnut to disguise the original strawberry color, although nothing could cover the explosion of freckles that blazed across her milk-white skin. Cameryn had known her for years. Although they weren't especially close, she liked Rachel. The only difficulty in dealing with her was that she tended to talk nonstop. Words poured out of her mouth in an uncensored cascade, which meant she spent half her life apologizing for what she said the other half of the time. And yet, no one ever really got mad at Rachel, because it was easy to read her heart. Cameryn herself often wished she was more free. She often felt she weighed her own words too carefully.

"Sorry if I offended you," Rachel told her now. "You know me and my mouth."

"No offense taken." Dipping her rag in her bucket once more, Cameryn concentrated on scrubbing a piece of petrified cheese stuck to the table's edge.

Rachel sighed. She walked to the end of the Grand and peered into the empty restaurant. She tapped her foot on the wooden floor and sighed again, louder this time. "It is so dead in here. Don't you think it's dead in here?"

"Yeah."

"Would you mind if I went home? My parents are out of town, which means I've got, like, a billion things to do, and I've made, like, five dollars in tips. There is absolutely no reason for two of us to be here, don't you think?"

That was true. Saturday afternoon sometimes dragged, but today's business had slowed to a crawl. The Grand usually served a light but steady tourist crowd, mostly families who had come up on the D & S train or kids who took up booths while splitting a single order of fries or cranky old-timers who demanded endless coffee refills. For some reason today's serving rooms remained empty.

"I was supposed to leave at seven," Cameryn said. "I've got plans for tonight."

"How about if I leave now and get back by then?"

"Sure," Cameryn said, nodding. "If George says it's okay, I'm fine with it."

But something new had caught Rachel's attention. A little bell jingled on the restaurant door as a man came in and strode to the bar. Plowing her hair back with her hand, Rachel stood, transfixed, as Justin Crowley straddled a round stool. They were in the back section of the restaurant, so they could watch, unnoticed.

"Ohmygosh, he *is* cute," Rachel breathed. "I heard he was, but . . ." She didn't finish her thought. It looked as though her entire body had gone on alert. As she stood staring, wide-eyed, Cameryn noticed the red-gold roots glinting at Rachel's scalp, like infinitesimal flames ready to catch the chestnut hair on fire. "Don't you think he's *cute*, Cameryn?"

"I don't know. He's okay, I guess," she replied.

"He's *way* better than okay. Hey, can I serve him? I mean, he *is* in your section and I *was* about to leave"—she looked at Cameryn eagerly—"but I could stay a little longer. The thing is, lately I've been attracting the absolute worst guys—it's like I've got some kind of loser radar or some-thing. I mean, guess who's been hanging around, trying to ask me out?"

"Who?"

"Adam the Freak. I've tried to be nice, you know, 'cause he's always alone and stuff, but that's where I went wrong. Now it's like he never gets the hint and I'm, like, 'Hello, go cast your spells on someone else,' but he just orders food and watches me. *That's* the caliber of guy I've been getting. But this deputy is totally fine. You don't mind if I give it a whirl, do you?"

With a dismissive wave of the hand, Cameryn said, "Be my guest."

"Thanks, Cammie—you're a true friend!" She flashed a smile over her shoulder as she made her way to the bar.

Cameryn squeezed the rag hard and watched as Rachel swooped in on her prey. Although the street outside was bright with four-o'clock sun, most of the Grand Hotel Restaurant seemed caught in a perpetual twilight. That was because the restaurant itself was a long, thin shoe box of a room, bisected into a larger back area for eating and smaller room in front for the bar. Daylight did not penetrate more than three feet from the restaurant's only window, and the rest of the fixtures—ten-inch hurricane lamps illuminated by electric candles—barely cast a glow. The hundred-year-old bar was the main attraction in the front room, which was where Crowley had settled himself. Carved with scrolls cut deep into mahogany, it stretched fifteen feet and boasted twelve stools. On the wall behind it hung a mirror, and directly above that was a bullet hole left there by Wyatt Earp himself, carefully circled so patrons would be sure not to miss that piece of the Grand's colorful past. A small television had been bolted to the wall, flashing pictures silently at the empty room.

She could hear Rachel's candied voice as she gave him a glass of water and began her usual small talk. Straining, she tried to decipher Justin's monosyllabic replies. Although the dried cheese had already been completely removed from the table, she continued to swipe it, her eyes focused on the rag while her whole mind concentrated on their hushed conversation. There was a clink of a glass, and then silence. Suddenly a shadow darkened; when Cameryn looked up she saw Rachel standing over her, her face twisted into an uncharacteristic frown. "He asked for you," she said curtly. "He says he wants you to wait on him."

"*Serve* him. Besides, who cares? You want him so you got him. Tell him I'm busy."

"That's a little hard to pull off when the restaurant's completely empty."

"He's your customer. I gave him to you."

"He's a customer who wants you, not me. By the way, you never told me you worked with him," she went on accusingly. "You never said he was there with the dead guy. Don't you think you should have mentioned it?"

"Why? He was there for, like, five minutes!"

"Whatever." Rachel sighed and shoved her order pad into her apron pocket. "Look, I'm going home. Just serve him and collect your tip, which I'm guessing is going to be huge since he's, like, 'I really want my waitress to be Cameryn.' I'll check with Callahan and if he says it's okay then I'm off, but I will return by seven! Have fun with your deputy." The sun had come out on her face again, and she gave Cameryn a knowing smile. Her voice suddenly became low, conspiratorial. "I don't care what you say—that guy's a definite hottie!"

And then she was gone. The saloon-type doors swung behind her as Rachel disappeared into the kitchen; the only sound was the wiper-like squeak of the hinges. There was nothing to do, Cameryn realized, but go and take the deputy's order. She walked slowly to the bar, trying hard to convey her annoyance. She could feel him watching her. Through the corner of her eye she saw that he had on regulation khakis and that his shirt was neatly tucked. His too-long hair, though, was tousled, as though he couldn't get the whole professional package quite right. The bangs brushed against his lashes like a dark curtain. His eyes met hers.

"Hi, Cammie," he said, gently thrusting his chin in her direction. "Good to see you again."

"What would you like?" Cameryn asked. She pulled out her pad and pencil, poised to write. Not that she needed it—she never wrote down an order for one. But the pad allowed her to keep her eyes off Justin's face. She didn't want to look at him.

"Well, to begin with," he said, "I'd like to be your friend."

His boldness startled her, and she couldn't help but look up. Justin's smile was back, only this time it appeared more like a Cheshire-cat grin.

"I meant to *eat*," she said. "What would you like to eat?"

"That other waitress was a pretty girl. Her name's Rachel, right?"

Cameryn didn't even bother to correct him on the term "waitress." Obviously, educating Justin was useless. He was a lost cause.

"But . . . I have to say you're even prettier. And you definitely have more fire."

"Look, are you going to order or not?"

"Okay, okay, just hold your horses—"

"*Hold your horses?* Uh, nobody talks that way around here, Justin. This may be the West, but we aren't living in some ancient *Gunsmoke* rerun!"

"I was trying to sound local."

"You sound stupid. Last chance to give me an order."

"Cheeseburger with fries and a Coke."

Scribbling furiously, Cameryn said, "Got it."

"Wait, don't go." Justin shifted forward on the barstool and rested his elbows on the bar's polished wood. Tracing his finger down the side of the sweating water glass, he asked, "Aren't you even a little bit curious about why I'm here?"

Cameryn flinched. She had wondered exactly that, but she didn't want him to know she was curious. Trying to keep from sounding too eager, she asked, "Um, is it to annoy me?"

"No. Actually, I'm here to *help* you."

"Oh, yeah. Right. I remember now," she said, nodding. "You've got a secret. But didn't you tell me I was a genius that had to figure it all out?"

His left eyebrow disappeared under his hair. "I did say that, didn't I?"

"You also said you were afraid of me."

This seemed to amuse him. "I don't remember that part."

"Doesn't matter—you said it."

"And why, exactly, would I be afraid of you?"

"Because you're the messenger. You said sometimes they kill the messenger. That would be me killing you, right?"

"Not to worry." He leaned forward and spoke softly, his

green-blue eyes dancing. "I think I'm ready to take my chances."

But he didn't get to say more. At that moment the bell on the door jingled again, and this time Sheriff Jacobs stepped inside. His boots made an ominous sound against the wooden floor as he stomped to the bar. In the backlight it was hard to read his features, although it was easy to read his voice.

"All right, Crowley, time's up," he said angrily. "We're supposed to be in Montrose right now. You can't just go off when the whim strikes you." Tugging on the bill of his sheriff's cap, he said, "Afternoon, Cameryn."

Justin stiffened. The tips of his ears flamed red while he sat, unmoving.

"Do you hear me, Deputy? I've been trying to find you for half an hour!"

"I thought I got a lunch break."

"Not when we're scheduled to leave town you don't."

Justin looked uncomfortable, and Cameryn felt embarrassed for him. "I'm sorry, Sheriff. I didn't check the board."

"Next time, look before you leave. Got that?"

"Of course." Justin swung his leg over the barstool and stood, his expression bland. "Guess we'll have to talk another time, Cameryn." Almost as an afterthought, he opened his wallet and dropped a ten-dollar bill on the counter. It lay there in jackknife position, still conforming to the shape of the billfold it had come from.

"I don't want—" she began to protest, but Justin shook his head.

"It's a down payment." It was more of a statement than a question, one that Cameryn wasn't required to answer. She thought about this as he left. Then, shrugging to herself, she picked up the money and dropped it into her apron pocket.

Chapter Four

"SO DID YOU WATCH *Shadow of Death* last night like you promised?" Lyric asked as she dumped her backpack into the backseat of Cameryn's Jeep. Next, she squeezed her ample frame into the passenger side and looked at Cameryn expectantly.

"No. I was going to." Cameryn tried to look convincing. "But then I had to help Mammaw in the kitchen and it just . . . slipped my mind."

"You are such a liar."

"What—why do you say that?" Cameryn asked.

"Because you are the absolute worst faker I have ever seen in my life. Your face goes red every time you tell a whopper, and right now you're the color of a brick. The truth is you promised to watch the show and you blew it off. Again. And you better hurry or we're going to be late for school. How I hate Mondays."

As usual, Lyric's blonde hair, now tipped with cobalt blue, had been woven into stubby braids that curled at her shoulders. Chunky boots made her taller than she already was. Her pants flared dramatically below the knee while her top, a hand-dyed T-shirt spun with brilliant psychedelic colors, hung past ample hips. She always dressed in the rainbow, from bright purples and oranges to bold magentas and greens. "It's my trademark," she'd say. "I match my color to my mood." She and Lyric had been best, if unlikely, friends ever since the day they'd first met.

Cameryn had been on her way to school, engrossed in avoiding stepping on the sidewalk cracks, when she noticed a house with colored beads hanging in the windows instead of curtains. She remembered thinking how pretty it was to have all those colors winking in the sunlight instead of the plain, heavy cloth her grandmother had put up. Just then the front door had swung open and Lyric had skipped out to greet her, as though she'd known her all her life. "Hi, I'm Lyric and I'm new," she'd said. "Are you on your way to school? 'Cause if you are, I'll walk with you." Cameryn had asked if she was a seventh-grader, but Lyric just laughed and said no, she was in fifth, she was just tall. "What grade are you in?"

"I'm in fifth, too," Cameryn replied. She'd hugged her books into her hollow chest while Lyric looked at her skeptically, an expression she had mastered even back then.

"No way! You're awfully little for a fifth-grader. Did they skip you ahead or something?"

"Nope."

Lyric had shrugged. "Well, you're the first person I've met who's my age. Maybe I can sit next to you in class."

"Maybe." This part Cameryn remembered clearly, since she didn't like being reminded of how small she was and she hadn't been at all sure she would like this moose of a girl. "But part of the time I'm in a different class." Stretching tall, she'd announced, "I'm in the gifted and talented."

"Cool! Me, too!" Lyric's face had erupted into a pudgy grin. "I'm glad that I'm smart, 'cause everybody always thinks I'm way older than I am. You know, I think it's a lot better to be like you and have people figure you're some kind of genius or something. So what's your favorite book?"

That's where it had begun, the against-the-odds friendship that had entwined them since childhood. Even though they looked, as her father put it, more like "owner and pet," they'd fought and laughed together like sisters, taking the same advanced classes while arguing over boys and music and the mystic. They were both only children who'd become pseudo-siblings, souls who saw the same world in very different ways. Like psychics, for instance. Lyric had total belief in them, while Cameryn thought they were nothing more than hacks in it for the money.

"Dang it!" Cameryn cried out now, barely missing a pothole that had appeared in the middle of Apple Street. All the roads save Greene Street were nothing but graded dirt, which meant small sinkholes and ruts could materialize overnight, like acne in reverse. She smacked the steering wheel with the palm of her hand and cried, "I wish the town council would shell out a couple of bucks and pave these side roads. I hate this."

"Smothering nature in asphalt isn't the answer."

"Neither is having my car realigned every six months. And if you're about to tell me I should embrace Mother Earth I will tell you to embrace the idea of walking to school."

"All right, all right, you win," Lyric said, frowning theatrically. "By the way, if you had watched *Shadow of Death* last night *like you promised*, you would have seen that Dr. Jewel himself spoke about a dirt road he saw somewhere in the mountains. And please don't roll your eyes when I'm speaking—that is completely rude."

Cameryn checked herself. "Sorry."

"To continue: Jewel said after the road-vision-thing, the spirit of a girl appeared to him—a girl from a place where the dirt road or path or whatever it was led straight to water. The dead girl told him her body was out there, lying facedown in the wild. It was *so* sad. Her spirit said she wasn't ready."

"And you believe this."

"Yes, Cameryn, I believe it!" Lyric's forehead wrinkled and her eyes, wide and rimmed in blue, were earnest. "She told him she was another victim of the Christopher Killer! Do you remember the Christopher Killer?"

Cameryn tried to feign interest in the case because Lyric *did* try to follow Cameryn and her forensic statistics. But paybacks were not fun. "Um, isn't the Christopher Killer the psychopath who leaves a Saint Christopher medal on the bodies?"

"Exactly. This one is, like, his fourth victim. See, Jewel always gets a message from the girls after they've been killed. The police listen to him. Lots of people believe he's real. I'm telling you, Cammie, the man is amazing."

Cameryn made another turn, past a home painted the color of cotton candy, one she had long ago dubbed the House of Pepto-Bismol. As she bumped past its neatly cropped lawn, festooned with a border of plywood flowers, she wondered at the human ability to have such faith in the artificial reality spun by Jewel and his kind. Like those wooden flowers, the fake stuff was perennial and impossible to kill.

"You have the strangest expression on your face," Lyric said. "What are you thinking?"

"You said Jewel saw mountains, a dirt road leading to water, and a body."

"Right."

"And you're not troubled by the fact that mountains

and dirt roads would be relevant in at least forty of our fifty states. Not to mention the fact that bodies statistically are almost always found near water." They were at Greene Street now, and when Cameryn stopped at a stop sign she could feel the heat of Lyric's look. Cameryn stole a glance at her: A strand of blue had curled itself across her cheek, which Lyric impatiently brushed away.

"You know what the real problem is?" Lyric asked.

"No, Lyric, what is the real problem?"

"The problem is my favorite show, *Shadow of Death*, is just not geeky enough for you."

"Yes. You are right. That would be the problem."

"Skeptic!"

"Sucker!"

They glared at each other, then dissolved into laughter because it was an old argument and one that would never be settled. Not that it had to be. They'd been friends long enough to be comfortable with each other's quirks. In their own ways they were both equally stubborn. Lyric had her crystals, Cameryn had her books, and in the end they honored their friendship treaty, the one they'd hammered out long ago.

Cameryn waited at the intersection as a few cars and a semitruck rumbled by. Down the street, the first shops were opening, their windows radiating butter-colored light onto the sidewalk, soft and inviting. The Steamin' Bean was opening its door, as was the Olde Silverton

Doughnut Shop. The town was waking up.

That's when Cameryn saw him. On the corner of Greene and Ore, a figure shuffled along the sidewalk, heading west. He was hunched in a black trench coat that reached to his ankles. A cigarette glowed from his fingertips. Black hair, flat and obviously dyed, hung to his shoulders, and his skin was Wonder-Bread white. He seemed to be watching his feet as they moved, although his head jerked up for just a moment as he crossed a street. Then he lowered his chin, took a drag off his cigarette, and resumed his foot-shuffle.

"Oooh, man, there he is," Lyric said softly. "Adam."

Cameryn made a *tsk*ing sound between her teeth. Although she hardly knew him, he always made her uneasy. "That is one strange kid," she said.

"Do you notice how he's always alone?" Lyric almost whispered, as though she were afraid of being overheard. "He's been alone ever since he moved here. I've tried to talk to him at school but it's gone nowhere. It's like he hates people or something."

"Did I tell you he's my lab partner?"

"No. Get out!"

"He doesn't really say anything to me, which is fine 'cause he reeks. He always smells like cigarettes."

They watched as Adam took another toke, exhaling through his nostrils as though he were a dragon. There had been rumors about him, whispers. He was a Satanworshipper who sacrificed small animals in secret blood rituals held deep in the woods, a Goth, a dangerous rebel, a drug addict. No one knew much about his father, except Lyric who, while working at her job at Ace Hardware, had sold him painting supplies.

"Adam doesn't have a mother," Lyric had reported. "I met his dad, though, and he had this scruffy beard and a long ponytail down to his waist. He told me he was an artist, but all he bought was regular house paint and great big brushes. What kind of art can you make with that?"

Like his father, Adam seemed to prefer solitude, eating by himself and studying in the farthest corner of the library. Maybe, in a larger city, a kid like Adam might have found his own, but not here. Silverton citizens would never embrace one so different from themselves.

"What do you say, Cammie?" Lyric asked her now. "Should we pick him up?"

Cameryn felt her blood stop. "Why?"

"I don't know," Lyric replied, shrugging. "Why not?"

"Don't tell me you like him."

"I didn't say that."

"'Cause he's got it for Rachel Geller. She told me he's been after her."

"Are you listening? I didn't say I *liked* him; I feel kind of sorry for him. Why shouldn't we give him a ride?"

"For one thing, he's smoking. You know I won't let anyone smoke in my car."

"He'll put it out."

"If we pick him up, our social stock will go down."

"Like we *have* any stock. Come on," she urged, "let's do a good deed. Just see if he'll ride with us."

But Cameryn just sat, watching him, her car idling. An instant later Lyric threw herself back into the seat.

"Okay, forget it," she said. "I was only thinking that if you put out good energy, good energy comes back." Lyric flipped down the visor, which signaled they were done, which irritated Cameryn. Her friend liked to take in strays, which was fine, but she always dragged Cameryn along for the ride.

"Sorry, I'm not doing it," Cameryn announced as she turned on to Greene Street.

"Whatever. It's your car, your karma."

"I don't believe in karma."

"Then knock some days off your time in purgatory."

"You're hilarious, Lyric. You know that?" Cameryn was determined to drive right by Adam but found herself slowing down as she approached him, her foot pressing on the brake pedal almost against her will. He must have sensed something, because for the briefest second he glanced at her. Adam was in front of the Grand now and he made a strange reflection in the plate glass window. It was an image from a funhouse mirror, white and black and wavering in the ancient glass, like an apparition. *At least he has a reflection,* she told herself. *That's a good thing.*

"Why do you *do* this to me?" she moaned as Lyric, sensing she'd won, pressed the button in the armrest. The window glided down and she leaned out on a meaty arm. "Hey, Adam," she said brightly.

Adam gave a terse nod and kept walking.

"You want a ride?"

He stopped. He took a drag and sent out an angry plume. "What for?"

"What do you mean, 'what for?' So you won't be late. You're not going to make it before the bell. Come on, hop in! But ditch the cigarette first, okay? No smoking in Cameryn's car. You know Cameryn."

"Yeah. We're lab partners."

Cameryn gave a friendly wave but his expression remained wary. In the gray light of morning, the paleness of his skin seemed even more pronounced. For a moment she thought he would refuse, but then he shrugged and flicked the cigarette into the gutter. With an expert motion he rubbed it beneath his sneaker and opened the back door to the car. He carried no backpack, which made Cameryn wonder where his books were. Although strange, he always seemed to do well in class. The smell of menthol infiltrated her car as Adam settled into the backseat; he spread his long, thin legs apart, his knees resting against both seatbacks. His coat hung open, revealing a black T-shirt, and a black leather cord with a miniature silver skull hung from his neck.

"Seat belt," Cameryn ordered.

"I don't believe in seat belts. I believe in fate. If we're meant to die, we die. If not, we live. Our lives are whatever is meant to be."

"If you're meant to ride in my car you buckle up," Cameryn shot back as she pulled onto Main. She caught his reflection in her rearview mirror, which revealed only a slash of his face. Adam kept his same, bland expression. "Whatever you say," he said, and snapped the buckle.

Lyric was all smiles as she twisted in the front seat, trying to make eye contact with Adam, chatting him up. For a while his replies were clipped. Cameryn was glad she had the job of driving since it gave her a cover for not really engaging in the conversation, freeing her to just listen.

At first he spoke in fits and starts, unused it seemed to conversation with kids his own age, but it didn't take long before he warmed up. It surprised Cameryn to hear Adam finally speak in more than a few clipped sentences. He had a good voice. It was deeper than she'd realized, supple in its rhythms, and it had a husky quality, probably, she guessed, from smoking.

"No matter where we move I always check out the cemeteries," he was saying. "The one here's a gold mine of oddities. Lots of funky people have been planted there," he told Lyric, who by now he was speaking to exclusively. "Reading tombstones is like reading a history book. Hey, see that shop—Silverton Souvenirs? I'm working there now."

"Really?" Lyric asked. "That's a cool place."

Cameryn knew the store. It was small, no more than fifteen feet wide, wedged between two refurbished eateries. Painted a dull olive, the Silverton souvenir shop had none of the charm of its neighbors. Tiny figurines crowded shelves along side racks crammed with cheap T-shirts stamped with the Durango & Silverton train. Behind the counter they sold souvenir spoons and matching teacups. To Cameryn, it was the equivalent of a town junk drawer.

"It's a dump. They sell all kinds of made-in-China crap, but it's got a mind-blowing basement. It's like a cave down there—earthen floors and walls and an old poker table from the twenties covered in a foot of dust. They got something else down there, too."

"What?"

Adam paused for effect. "A ghost. A prostitute who was murdered around eighty years ago. My boss says she won't leave until her body is found. But if someone *did* find her body, it won't be much—by now it'd just be a skull and maybe a couple of bones."

"No way!" Lyric cried. "Are you serious? Cameryn, did you hear that? There's a ghost in the basement of the souvenir shop."

"Oh, yeah," Cameryn replied, "I heard it." She had sudden clarity as to Lyric's motives concerning Adam. Wacky people are always drawn to their own kind.

"Cameryn doesn't believe in ghosts," Lyric said smugly, "but I do."

Adam nodded in her rearview mirror. "Science-types only believe their five senses, totally ignoring their sixth one."

"Hello, I'm in the car!" Cameryn interjected. She was suddenly feeling left out. "Please don't talk about me like I'm not here."

He leaned forward, his chin between the backs of the bucket seats. "No disrespect intended," he told her. "My point is I'm not afraid to say I'm a believer. There is more to this world than what we see. When I went to the grave-yard I swear I saw a black shape move through the tomb-stones. It freaked me out. I mean, I actually saw this *thing*—a being from the other side. Just last night I was watching *Shadow of Death*—"

Lyric hit Cameryn's thigh but said nothing.

"—and man, Jewel just blew me away. This girl's spirit was talking right to him. And what's really whacked is I started wondering if the murdered girl was killed some-where around here. The way he described the mountains made me think of Silverton. We could have had a murder in our own little town."

"Oh, come *on!*" Cameryn let out a derisive snort. "Why would a serial killer come to dinky Silverton? That's completely insane. We don't have murders here."

That was true. When Silverton was a frontier town, people were shot all the time, but the violence had dried up since it entered respectability. Her father had told her of a case, barely within Cameryn's memory, where a wife caught her drunk of a husband cheating and split his skull with a meat cleaver. Patrick said the town felt the jerk had it coming, the judge gave the wife a light sentence, and that was the end of violent crime in Silverton.

"I would have agreed with you right up until I saw the show, which—check this out—he did live," Adam replied. "Jewel said he saw orange soil and mountains. Think about the soil around here. It's, like, the color of pumpkins."

"That's true!" Lyric chimed. "I forgot about that part. Jewel did say he saw the color orange."

"You both are delusional." Cameryn was relieved to be turning into the parking lot of Silverton's one and only school. It was an old building with arced windows and stone sconces. Since the school housed kids of all ages, she had to be especially careful driving into the school zone. Kids on bikes bumped along the sidewalks on their way to the elementary wing, their jackets zipped snug around eager faces. Older kids walked in clumps. The small parking lot was already overflowing with vehicles, mostly four-wheel drives and pickup trucks, a staple of those accustomed to mountain living.

As she looked at the cars and the flushed faces of the kids, she realized that *this* was her reality. Real people contained in real bodies going to a real school made of brick. Of course she had her faith, but hers was old and rooted in time, ancient in its rhythms and as immovable as stone. The saints might intercede when summoned, but the rest of the dead were busy in heaven doing whatever it was souls did, and Cameryn liked the division. It was as clear as the separation between day and night. In her daylight hours, science ruled and questions had absolute answers, while in her nighttime world of faith, candles smoked, wafting prayers into paradise. It was a comfortable partition.

In Cameryn's reality the dead did not get channeled into mediums, they did not haunt station wagons, and they did not show themselves to psychics who charged money for the privilege of telling those who grieved that souls of their loved ones were blissfully happy as they took the next step on their journeys.

"Cameryn looks a bit peeved," Lyric said.

"No, Cameryn is feeling outnumbered," Cameryn replied, easing into a parking space. "And Cameryn is tired of this conversation." Lyric was just starting to protest when Cameryn heard her cell phone ringing from her back pocket, playing thin, high notes from the *Lord of the Rings* movie. Shifting her hip forward, she retrieved her phone and looked at the number. It was her father.

"Hey, Dad," she said. "What's up?"

"Can you get away from school?" He sounded harried. "I'll write a note. I need you right now."

"Sure. First period is just my study hall. I'm not even inside—I'm still in my car."

"Stay there. You're in the parking lot, right? I'll pick you up."

It was the tone in his voice that made her heart jump. "What's going on? Is it Mammaw?"

Even over the phone she could hear him quaver. "They've . . . some hikers found a body. By the stream near Smith Fork."

It seemed as though the interior of her Jeep became a shade darker, as though the upholstery had suddenly absorbed more light. Her mouth moved but no sound came out.

"It's the body of a girl."

"What is it?" Lyric whispered. Cameryn shook her head and pressed her finger in her ear. "What girl?" she asked. "Do they know who it is?"

"Not yet. The sheriff can't touch the body until we're there."

"Does it look like it was an accident?"

"Just stay in the parking lot until I arrive." He took a deep, wavering breath. "Cammie . . . the sheriff says it's murder."

Chapter Five

"YOU GUYS DON'T HAVE TO wait here with me," Cameryn said, drumming the steering wheel nervously. "The bell's going to ring any second, and . . . I don't know, I just . . ." She didn't finish the sentence. It felt like she couldn't string her words together, or worse, her thoughts. It was hard to make anything inside her head line up. Instead, her syllables spun like autumn leaves caught in a whirligig of air. It was all the crazy talk of Jewel that was making her think sideways. She had to pull herself together.

"Don't worry about me; I don't care if I'm late," Adam announced from the backseat. "I mean, I'm still trying to take it all in. Somebody's dead." He shook his head and exclaimed, "Man. It's just like Jewel said last night."

"We don't know that—right now we don't know anything

except someone died. And, you guys know not to say anything to anyone at school, right?" Cameryn said for the third time. "Remember, my dad said he didn't want reporters showing up. It's still a crime scene. We've got to get it all sorted out."

"We already promised we wouldn't say a word," Lyric replied. "Don't worry, we'll keep our mouths shut. But, you do realize this is going to be a Christopher killing. When the media catches wind of what happened, it's going to get crazy. You need to prepare yourself."

"It's *not* the Christopher Killer," Cameryn said, her voice sharp. "Okay, it's a possible murder—and I say possible because we haven't even been to the scene yet to know for sure—but that doesn't mean it's *the* murder. I mean, you just made a huge leap in logic. I want to stick to facts."

"The fact is this—a murdered girl in the mountains is just what Dr. Jewel saw in his vision," Lyric told her calmly. "The orange soil. The body by water. I don't care if you believe me now or not, because you will believe as soon as you get there."

But Cameryn would hear none of it. "Statistically, there have been lots of murders since Jewel made his prediction. And by the way, where was Dr. Jewel when he 'saw' all this, anyway?"

"New Mexico," Adam answered. From his coat pocket he pulled out a cigarette and rolled it between his hands. Cameryn turned in her seat so she could watch him.

"You're not going to light that, are you?" she asked.

Adam shook his head. "See, right now Jewel's holding a live psychic convention down there in Santa Fe. But you can't let the distance throw you, because with mediums, space and time and all of those existential limitations no longer exist. It's still hard to get my head around this. I knew Jewel had power, but I got to admit this is freaking weird." He stopped rolling his cigarette and looked up through his curtain of hair. "Do you think the dead girl is someone from Silverton?"

Her heart skipped a beat. "No way," she said. Cameryn didn't know why she was so sure, but she was. "It's got to be a tourist. We've still had a lot of people coming up on the train since the weather's been so good. It'll be an out-of-towner. And I'm getting out of the car—I think I need some air."

As if on cue, the three of them spilled out of the car. It was harder for Adam. He exited legs-first, unfolding himself, piece by piece, as though he were a piece of collapsible gear that needed to be reassembled outside its box. Lyric reached around him to grab her backpack, and when she did, she accidentally bumped against him.

"Sorry," she said softly.

Crossing her arms, Cameryn leaned against the side of the Jeep and waited. It was only eight thirty and already the air was warming up. October weather in Silverton could be schizophrenic. The last few days had brought cool temperatures in the mornings and evenings only, when the sky was still purple-blue and the stars mere pricks of pale light. The middle of the day, however, had been uncharacteristically warm. The higher than normal temperatures, she knew, would make her father's job—her job—that much harder.

She knew a body would decompose fast in the heat. Insects, especially blowflies, honed in on their mark within hours and laid their eggs into any available flesh. That was the science of it. A short while later maggots would emerge, a wriggling white mass capable of stripping a corpse to the bone within weeks, depending on temperature and humidity levels, which meant precious evidence could be lost quickly.

And that wasn't even factoring in the animal activity that would inevitably occur when a body was left in the wild. Mentally she tried to prepare herself for what she might see, but how could she steel her insides for what lay at Smith Fork? Was it only last week that she'd seen the man in the bathtub? It seemed like a lifetime ago that she'd retched from the smell. Today, Cameryn realized, could be much, much worse.

Adam lit his cigarette with a plastic lighter, politely blowing the smoke away from Cameryn. His smoking irritated her. She wished the two of them would leave, but at the same time she liked them there with her—just one more contradictory set of emotions to sort through. The warning bell rang, followed by the bell signaling the start of school, and still her father had not come.

"What's taking your dad so long?" Lyric asked, tapping her foot into the dirt. "I thought he was rushing right over to pick you up."

Cameryn shrugged. "He might have stopped to get a white body bag. They're supposed to use white ones when it's a murder. That's what the books say, anyway."

"Why white?" Adam asked. Already he was working on a second cigarette. A bit of paper had stuck to his bottom lip, which he carefully pinched off.

"Because evidence left inside the bag is easier to spot."

Adam nodded. He took a drag and exhaled. "Man, how do you *know* this stuff?"

"I read," she answered. "I study. I focus on things you can see, taste, smell, and test. Then I throw in a rosary for Mammaw and I'm good to go."

"And they say *I'm* twisted."

At that moment Patrick's station wagon whipped around the corner and into the parking lot. From the way he clutched the steering wheel she could tell he was upset.

"Dad!" she cried, waving frantically. "Over here!"

When he saw her he flipped a U-turn in front of the school, so close his wheel bounced up on the curb. He slowed down as he approached them. The passenger-side window was already down, and he scooped the air with his hand, ordering her in. "Come on, they're waiting for us!"

A jolt of electricity shot through Cameryn as she hopped inside the car and buckled up. Adam and Lyric gave a wave as the station wagon pulled away. She watched them as they grew smaller in the distance, Adam, as tall and thin as a poplar tree next to Lyric's full evergreen frame. Lyric's backpack slumped between them like a tired dog.

The station wagon turned onto Greene, and soon the car was heading south along the Million Dollar Highway, so named because it cost the state well over a million dollars to carve it into the high mountains. Patrick said nothing; his posture behind the wheel was ramrod straight, and his head grazed the ceiling of the car, bending his hair back like the bristles of an old scrub brush.

"I'm sorry to make you miss school," he said. "I almost didn't call you, but since it's a murder, well, I need all the help I can get."

"It's okay, Dad. You know I've got all As. So do they know who it is?" she asked.

Patrick shook his head. "Not yet. With all the tourists running around it's most likely one of them and . . . well, it's bad no matter who it is, right? Jacobs said the victim appears young." Shaking his head, he looked as though he were trying the clear his thoughts. "But we've got to get to business. I've brought two cameras—one'll take color and the other black and white. So here's what I want you to do: I want you to photograph the body from every conceivable angle using both the cameras—color first. That'll be important." He rubbed a hand over his chin. "It's been years since I've done homicide and I'm trying to remember every single step. The cameras and other supplies are in that knapsack in the back. Can I put you in charge?"

Cameryn nodded. She'd taken many photographs in her life, just never of something so grim.

"Good. I've got to admit it, I'm glad you're with me." He wore a long-sleeved plaid shirt beneath a navy bomber jacket. Patrick tugged at the collar of his shirt and then, with one hand, unfastened the top button. "The way you handled yourself with Robertson, Cam, well, you were a real professional. I have total faith in you. And it sure doesn't hurt that you've been reading up on forensics. I could use some of that expertise."

If she hadn't been so preoccupied with the murder she might have cringed at the compliment. When faced with Robertson's body the second time around she'd been able to hold her emotions in check. The difference was in knowing what was in front of her, of being mentally steeled. Stone-faced, she'd photographed the body, and both her father and Jacobs thought her a natural investigator, which she'd let them believe. And Justin, true to his promise, never said a word. But that was a different death, a different reason. This was a murder.

Now they fell into silence. She looked out of the station

wagon, to the pines that marched straight up the granite mountain in an endless evergreen army. The trees were thick at Smith Fork, and Cameryn suddenly wondered if there was blood there. And if that blood soaked into the earth to disappear like water into sand, what then? Were they supposed to dig it out? Her books hadn't told her anything about that—they probably hadn't told her about a lot of things. She pictured blood and suddenly she had a strange thought: What happened to the blood they couldn't reach? Would the tree roots drink up the blood molecules? If the roots leeched the blood, then the victim might become part of the trees themselves and live again, like the circle of life that Lyric always talked about.

Or was it like her mammaw told her—when you died, your spirit soared to heaven and you lived on streets paved with gold? Or were you just dead, like the deer she saw strapped to big pickup trucks that rumbled through Silverton every fall.

Robertson had looked plain dead. The old lady had looked peaceful, sleeping, and thinking of that face Cameryn could believe in some kind of angelic rest. But what happened with a murder, when a soul was ripped out of a body and the person wasn't ready? Cameryn squeezed her eyes shut; it seemed as though her mind was jumping sideways again. She had to get a grip, to think clinically instead of emotionally. She'd be no good at all if she didn't get her thoughts clear.

On her right she saw a sheet of water weeping from slick rock, and past that a wall of stone where the mountain had been sheared off as if by a giant's knife. Smith Fork, and the body it contained, was less than a mile ahead. She chewed on the edge of her lip.

"You're mighty quiet there, Cammie."

"I was just thinking."

"About what?"

"Something Lyric told me. She said a psychic in New Mexico talked to the spirit of a girl who was murdered near a stream, and now this has happened, and, well . . ." She looked at him, eyes wide. "Dad, do you think . . . ?"

"There are lots of murders and lots of streams. The only fact that's real is that there's a dead girl out there. Lyric's a sweetheart and I love her, but don't be dancing to her song. One colorful seventeen-year-old in Silverton's enough. And who was that other kid with you? I don't remember seeing him before."

"His name's Adam."

"Oh, so that's Adam. I've heard about him."

"Tell me about Sheriff Jacob's call," she said, changing the subject. "I figure it can't be one of us locals or he'd have identified her."

"Except the victim's lying facedown."

"Didn't he turn her over?"

"No. Remember, he can't move the body until I get there."

Cameryn swallowed. "Was she shot?"

"Doesn't appear so. Jacobs said he didn't see any obvious signs of trauma."

"Well if she's facedown and there's no bullet hole then how does he know it's a murder?"

Her father waited a beat before replying, "Her hands were tied behind her back. Duct tape."

"Oh," she said. Picturing it, she felt almost paralyzed inside. "Well."

"Oh well is right, Cammie. From this point on everything we do will become evidentiary, which means there'll be a lot of pressure to do it right. Obviously, there will be an autopsy. And even though I know it'll be hard, I'll say it again—I'm mighty glad to have you with me. You've got great instincts." Her father glanced at his watch. "It's been over half an hour since the call came in. Jacobs is having a fit while he waits on me, but, technically I own the body so he's stuck till I show. I'll have to buy him a beer when it's over."

"A beer?" Cameryn's eyes widened. "It's still morning!"

"It won't be when we're done. We won't be getting the body to Durango before three o'clock."

Hesitating, she asked, "Is Deputy Crowley with him?"

Her father's voice cooled. "Don't know. I didn't ask."

Patrick took a hard right onto a narrow dirt road, one Cameryn wasn't sure the station wagon could easily handle. Had it only been this morning that she'd complained about Silverton's dirt roads? Those streets in town were graded almost every month in order to remain smooth and hard-packed, but Smith Fork was one step from wild. Now she bumped along like a rodeo rider on a bull, pitching back and forth so hard her teeth jarred. If they had to park and walk, it would take time, and, Cameryn realized, it would be harder still to carry the body back to their wagon on a stretcher.

She need not have worried, though, because soon the sheriff's SUV loomed into view. His lights were flashing blue and red onto a knot of people who stood to one side. A woman with a blanket around her shoulders looked like she was crying while Justin, pad and pen in hand, scratched down information.

After he parked, her father pulled a large case from the bay of the station wagon while Cameryn grabbed the black knapsack from the backseat. When they shut the car doors, the sound echoed off the face of a nearby mountain; it sounded like gunshots.

Yellow tape had been tied to the base of some trees in a huge, lopsided square, at least four hundred feet on each side including the opposite side of the stream. In the square, standing dead center was John Jacobs. His body was positioned at an odd angle. Leaning forward from his waist, hands pressed to his face, his elbows akimbo like a pair of coat hangers, he held something to his eye.

Cameryn quickly realized he held a camera, but she could see only a patch of wheatgrass shimmering in the sun. The body must have been directly beneath Sheriff Jacobs's camera lens.

"John, we're here," her father called, waving his arm.

Sheriff Jacobs looked up, acknowledged their presence with a quick nod, then went back to snapping pictures.

Their shoes scuffed through the dirt as they made their way toward the crime scene. Two women dressed in hiking gear stood miserably to one side, waiting for the woman in the blanket to finish with Crowley. They eyed Cameryn as she got closer but said nothing. Cameryn could hear the woman in the blanket speak between sobs.

" . . . and then there she was! I almost walked right on top of her when I saw her leg and at first I thought it was just a mannequin. Then I realized it was a real person and so me and my friends, we called 911 right away—thank God we had a cell phone—and then Sophie started to faint and Amanda caught her. I mean you see death on television but it's different when it's real. That girl—just lying there facedown in the dirt. How could anyone do this to another human being? It's terrible . . . just terrible." The woman blew her nose, and Crowley patted her shoulder awkwardly. He looked at Cameryn, but Cameryn pretended not to see. She was still embarrassed from their last meeting, and more than a little intrigued. It was best not to let him know, so she kept her gaze straight ahead.

They were only twenty feet away from Sheriff Jacobs when Cameryn heard Justin call out to her father.

Patrick stopped and Cameryn stopped with him. Turning abruptly, her father said, "Yes?"

The wind had been blowing, which caused Crowley's hair to fall across his forehead in tousled locks. He jerked his head at Cameryn. "Sir, do you think this is wise?"

"Excuse me, I'm doing my job," Cameryn replied, annoyed by his condescension. "I'm assistant to the coroner, remember?"

Crowley kept his gaze on her father. "I'm sure you already realize that this isn't a natural—we're dealing with a murder. I think it's too strong for the young lady to see."

"Young *lady*?" Now she was indignant. "Are you serious?"

Her father's eyes flashed. "What I do with my own family is none of your concern, Deputy, although you seem to think otherwise. My daughter is here in an official capacity. Now if you'll excuse us, we've got work to do. I suggest you do the same. Come on, Cammie."

Justin dug his hands into his pockets. "All right, all right, I understand, but I just need to speak to Cameryn for just one—"

"I said we're done!" Her father bit off every word.

Patrick marched ahead and jerked up the yellow tape, allowing Cameryn to duck under first. With a smooth motion he slid under as well, leaving Justin on the other side. She wanted him to stay there. There was not enough room in her head to deal with murder and Justin Crowley so she let the yellow ribbon do the work for her. Thoughts of Justin would stay on the other side of her mind, cordoned off by the strip of plastic tape. There was no more room for games.

"Don't get too close to the body until I tell you," Patrick warned. "From now on everything counts."

Cameryn said nothing. She was glad he couldn't hear the hammering of her heart. Twenty feet away a murder victim lay in the grass, and Cameryn was part of the case, a part of the team that could put the pieces together. It was exhilarating and terrifying at the same time. She could feel her hands begin to tremble so she clenched them, hard. This was what she'd been working for, what she'd wanted. Blowflies buzzed through the grass like tiny vultures while birds chirped overhead, ready to eat the flies that ate the girl. Cameryn steeled herself now; she was a link in the chain that would hang the criminal who did this, and she was glad.

And then she saw the body.

The first thing she noticed were the shoes—regular Nikes like Cameryn and all her friends wore, but the girl's feet seemed especially awkward, as if she were a ballerina dancing on pointe. The victim's hands had been tied behind her with duct tape, and her fingers, white as marble, curled like claws. Long, brown hair ended in the middle of her back in a perfect line, as if it had been combed after death, and her face was hidden by a fringe of wild grass. She wore jeans and a T-shirt. A bracelet twinkled from her wrist. From her size and the kind of clothes she wore, Cameryn guessed her to be about her age. About her age and dead. A chill spread inside her and she looked at the grass near her feet.

"Took you long enough," was Sheriff Jacobs's greeting. "I didn't touch the body, didn't even go into her pockets. We need to go by the book."

"Let me get some pictures before we move anything. Cammie?"

At the sound of her name, Cameryn snapped her head up.

"Start with color."

"Oh. Right. Sure."

Numb, Cameryn reached into the knapsack and brought out the Canon. Focusing on the shoes, she began to snap one picture, then another, like an automated robot. Emotions surged through her in rapid succession—horror, fascination, fear, curiosity, and yet most of all anger. It welled up like bile in her throat—no one deserved to die this way, trussed like an animal and left in the wild. *Snap, snap, snap.* She began to take the pictures more rapidly now.

"Did you get an ID on her?" Cameryn's father asked Jacobs.

"I already told you I didn't touch her. Procedure, remember?"

"Uh-huh. I think I need to bag her hands before we do anything else. I don't want to lose trace evidence."

Patrick placed a medium-sized paper bag around the victim's hands and secured it with a large rubber band. He had to use paper, Cameryn knew, because plastic could cause any trace evidence to degrade.

More pictures, and then Cameryn switched to the black-and-white. Her father and the sheriff talked and wrote down notes. Deputy Crowley was beginning to sweep the grass with a metal detector, his brow furrowed in concentration. Police from Durango were on the way to help secure the crime scene, Jacobs told them, and they'd have more folks sweeping for whatever they could find. The three women stood at the yellow tape line, watching, like cattle behind a fence. Her father put on gloves and searched the girl's back jeans pockets for ID but found nothing; finally he declared it was time to roll the body over. By now, Deputy Crowley had joined them. He tried to look at Cameryn, but she refused to meet his gaze.

"Ready?" her father asked.

Jacobs nodded and placed his hands carefully under the corpse's shoulders while Justin put his hands beneath her hip. Her father held the head.

"One, two, three!" Patrick said. "Careful, now."

The body was stiff, in full rigor, and as it rolled the hair fell forward to cover the face in a chestnut-colored web; gently, her father removed it, and then his eyes grew wide. "Oh, no," he said. "Oh, God, please no."

And then Cameryn saw the perfect oval face and the eyes staring blankly, and she felt her hand fly to her mouth and tears blurred her vision until she couldn't see anymore.

"Oh, my God!" she cried. "That's Rachel!"

Chapter Six

THE MEDICAL EXAMINER'S BUILDING looked nothing like Cameryn expected. Located at the south end of Durango, it was an unassuming red-brick rectangle with a flat gravel roof, as plain and utilitarian as a Laundromat. Adjacent to the back end of the Mercy Medical Center, the building had two metal garage doors and only one small window facing the parking lot. Cameryn would not have even noticed it save for the small sign that read, in plain block letters, COLORADO STATE MEDICAL EXAMINER. Turning the car around, her father backed the station wagon until it almost touched the garage door and tapped his horn twice. He'd called from the road and they knew he was coming.

"You sure you're all right?" her father asked her again. "The way you're just sitting there, staring into space, well,

I'm starting to think . . . Why not pass on the autopsy, Cammie? Go get yourself something to eat. You proved how useful you can be with Robertson but . . . this isn't about me anymore. I want to do what's best for you."

"I'm fine," she said flatly.

"I'd believe it except for the fact that you haven't spoken two words to me the whole ride down."

"That's because I've been thinking."

"About Rachel?"

Cameryn nodded. What else would she be thinking about?

"It's always worse when you know them, baby," he told her softly, and she could feel his hand on her arm, firm and comforting. "The question is, do you still want to do this job?"

"Yes."

"Then you've got to learn to detach. It's the only way to survive."

"I understand," she said. She looked at him, tears welling in her eyes. "But how am I supposed to *do* it?"

"By remembering that if we do our job right we'll find out who did this and bring him to justice. We're the last line of defense for the victim. You're the one who said the dead tell their stories to us." He put his finger under her chin and pulled her face up. "We've got to keep it together for Rachel's sake. Focus on that, and you'll get through."

"I keep thinking that this is the last—" The words caught in her throat. She swallowed, then went on haltingly, "The *only* thing I can do for her now."

Her father gave a faint nod and said nothing more. Turning from him, Cameryn pressed her forehead against the car window's cool glass and watched as a band of small brown birds pecked the asphalt with their yellow beaks. This death felt so different from the bloated stranger in a bathtub. The old, the sick, the drug addicts—they died. She didn't like it but she could accept it. But this was someone she knew in life, and there was no way to make sense of it.

Only last week Rachel had been talking about moving to Durango so she could attend college there. She'd graduated in June but, without enough money, had been forced to stay another year in Silverton to save up.

"I figure I'll have enough in my account by August," she'd said. "Rich kids get a pass but me, I got to work for it. But the way I figure, in less than a year I'll be living in the dorms and out on my own. It's all in front of me," she'd said, eager, "you know?"

The only thing that had been waiting for her was a white body bag. Wrapping her in a plain cotton sheet, Cameryn and her father had slipped Rachel into the vinyl carrier and zipped her up like garments in a suitcase. They'd wheeled her to the back of the station wagon, the wheel protesting loudly, and then they'd slammed the door shut. For some reason the slamming of the door had made Cameryn want to cry. She hadn't, though, remembering a trick Rachel had taught her when she'd burned her palm on the griddle. "If you think you're going to cry, then look up at the ceiling," she'd instructed Cameryn. "No one will ever know you're crying if you just look up."

The birds outside the car window blurred. Cameryn looked up just as the garage door rolled open. A thickly muscled black man in green medical scrubs waved for them to back in, and moments later her father parked and the man unlatched the station wagon hatch.

"Hey, Pat," he said. "Man, we've already had a bunch of calls on this one—media's going wild. Oh, I'm supposed to tell you Sheriff Jacobs and his deputy are on their way and he's sorry they got delayed. What's the vic's name?"

"Rachel Geller, eighteen," her father said. "Hiker stumbled on her body at approximately oh–six hundred hours. Best guess is she died around midnight. From the petechial hemorrhaging in the eyes I'd say a ligature strangulation. There's bruising on her neck, too."

Shaking his head, the man said, "Poor child. Let me give you a hand and we'll get her inside."

Once again, Rachel's body was lifted onto the gurney. Cameryn put her hands under the bag and helped to lift it, and even through the white vinyl she could tell Rachel was softening. She must have been entering the second stage of rigor mortis.

"Whoa, wait a minute, who's this?" the man asked when he realized Cameryn was sharing the load.

"I'm sorry, I should have introduced you. Ben, this is my daughter Cameryn. Cameryn, this is Ben Short—he's the diener."

Cameryn knew a diener was someone who assisted the pathologist with his most gruesome jobs, including the repackaging of organs into the body cavity and washing the corpse before sending it on to the funeral home. It was a tough job, but Ben seemed almost jovial until his dark eyes bored into hers. The smile drained from his face. "She can't come in here, Pat. This is a homicide."

"Cameryn's my assistant," her father answered. "Don't worry, the job gives her clearance. She's got a good eye and I'm grateful for her help."

"Okay, if you say so." Ben still looked doubtful. His eyes seemed to register her jeans and pink hoodie, her dirty sneakers and her plastic mood ring. She wished she hadn't worn her hair in a ponytail. "Just for a heads-up," Ben said, "Moore's in a foul mood today. So—it's Cameryn, right?"

She nodded.

"A word to the wise: Stay out of his way and keep quiet. The man does not suffer fools."

"That works 'cause neither do I."

As Ben's face split into a wide smile, she noticed he had beautiful teeth. "So you're trash-talking, are you?

That's good, girl. You've got some spunk. But we'll see how you do when the dragon master shows. All right, you two—follow me. We got to take this body to the chop shop." He squeezed his eyes shut, then looked at Cameryn apologetically. "Sorry—sometimes we use gallows humor around here. What I meant to say is we'll take Ms. Geller down to the autopsy suite. We got one stop to make first."

Since her father and Ben could handle the gurney, Cameryn hung back as they wheeled Rachel down the long hallway. The building looked like a regular office, with plain brown carpeting and motel art hanging on the walls. But the air had a faint, oppressive odor, the same smell she'd encountered at the Silverton Motel— except this time it was masked by a layer of disinfectant. Still, the patina of death overshadowed the scent of Lysol and bleach. Cameryn wondered if it had seeped into the building's very walls.

A door was open on her right, and as she passed it she peered inside. It was a small room. Three brown chairs with metal legs were arranged in a half-circle. There was a shelf holding a box of Kleenex. It made her shudder to think of those who would go in there to wait for news that was never good, and her mind flashed to Rachel's parents. Who would tell them their daughter was dead? *Don't go there,* she told herself. *Not now.* Another door on her left said HISTOLOGY LAB and a third, unmarked door remained closed. Her father and Ben were waiting for her in the hallway.

"Here we are. Our first stop," Ben announced. He knocked the bar handle with his hip as he stepped into a room so small it seemed no bigger than a closet. Cameryn crowded in beside him while her father stayed in the hall.

Ben said, "First, we x-ray. Some MEs—that's what we call the medical examiner—some of them x-ray the body after it's been processed. Down here in Durango we film straight through the bag. Makes it easier when they're still wrapped up nice."

The machine was large, with a movable arm that ended in a flat plate. "Won't the bag's zipper screw up the shot?" Cameryn asked, imagining a jagged, impenetrable line running across the picture.

Ben looked pleased. "Your daddy's right—you are a smart girl. But this here body bag is done in what's called an envelope-style, and what we got to do is put the arm of the machine between the deceased and the bag. Then I'll zap her with both an anterior and a posterior shot, which means we'll be able to see everything just fine."

She tried not to wince at the casual way he referred to "zapping" Rachel, but she knew people in the forensics used humor to cope. Someday she, too, would be cutting into bodies, and it wasn't hard to imagine she would make light of it. Right now it felt too raw, too real. "Why an X-ray?" she asked, trying to keep her mind focused.

"Won't the autopsy itself show everything we need?"

Ben blew out a breath. "Well, there are lots of things the X-ray'll catch that the plain eye could miss. Now, if this was, say, a gunshot victim, and he got hit right under the right armpit"—Ben touched the area beneath his arm—"that bullet could end up just about anywhere inside the body. I've found 'em all the way down in the groin and shot up in the head and in all sorts of strange locations. So if we do the X-ray first, then that bullet will show up on film like a big old star, which means Dr. Moore won't have to wade through the guts to find it through the trajectory path. Make sense?"

"But she wasn't shot."

"We don't know anything for sure. If she was strangled the X-ray might reveal some damage to the interior structure of the neck. Now I'm gonna ask you to wait outside for safety reasons—radiation and all of that. In a few minutes I'll wheel her back out and we'll go on down to the suite. This won't take long," Ben told her, and the door clicked shut behind her.

For a moment her father didn't say anything and Cameryn thought he wasn't going to. But he leaned close and whispered, "How you holding up?"

"I'm still here." Her eyes brimmed with tears. "It's hard, because one minute I feel like I'm blown away by the process and the next I feel like I'm being punched in the gut. I keep thinking she's only one year older than I am, and it could have been me out in that field. What are her parents going to do without her? What am *I* going to do?"

Patrick looked at the floor. He wore heavy leather work boots, and he kicked his heel against the brick wall. "You never know what fate has in store for any of us."

"Fate?" Cameryn glared him and at the thought. "Evil trumps fate. I mean, a week ago Rachel told me her life was all in front of her but now she's got nothing." Suddenly she clutched her father's hand. "You think there's a heaven?" she asked. "Right? You believe, don't you?"

"Of course there's a heaven," he said, pulling her close.

"What about hell?"

He waited a beat before saying, "I don't know. Maybe. Maybe it'll be like your mammaw says, with all that fire scorching the bad people for eternity, although up until now I thought hell is what we give each other here on earth."

"Well I hope Mammaw's right," Cameryn said fiercely. "I hope whoever did this will burn *forever*!"

Patrick didn't answer this. Instead, he rested his head on the brick and searched the ceiling. "I can't even imagine what the Geller family is going through right this very minute. Jacobs said he'd go tell the parents. They were at a friend's cabin and there was no cell-phone service so they couldn't call home. The Gellers didn't even realize Rachel was gone." He pinched the bridge of his nose and closed his eyes. He looked older somehow. The skin beneath his eyes creased more than she remembered while his neck was seamed beneath his ears. Pressing his back against the wall, he crossed his arms and sighed, and she did the same. There was a sudden weariness that seemed to wrap around her bones and then she realized the energy it took to keep her emotions in check. It was hard to remember that Rachel was no longer Rachel—she was now evidence in a crime.

The door swung opened as Ben pushed the gurney out feet-first, executing a perfect right-face into the hall. "All right folks, we're going to those big double doors. I gave Moore a buzz and he says he'll be there in a few minutes. Right this way."

Cameryn trotted after him, surprised at how fast he could move while pushing a body. With his hip he smacked into a set of swinging doors and she and her father stepped in quickly after him. The autopsy suite itself was huge, the size of at least ten of her bedrooms, and yet it seemed strangely empty. Sounds echoed off sterile surfaces like sonar pings. Overhead fluorescent lights cast a harsh glow on the green-and-white tile, and three steel autopsy tables lay in wait next to two cavernous stainless steel sinks. Cameryn couldn't help but notice the smell was worse here. She began to breathe through her mouth as Ben wheeled the gurney next to the closest table.

"Mind if you-all help me move her?" he asked.

Cameryn grabbed a white handle on the body bag while her father took the feet. On the count of three they carefully slid Rachel onto the table.

"Thanks," Ben grunted. "You've met Moore before, right, Pat?"

"Yep. Is he still a pompous windbag?"

Cameryn shot her father a look.

"Let's just say he's still my boss," Ben answered carefully. "Cameryn, I don't think he's going to let you stay. Just be ready for a fight. The man runs a tight ship."

"*I'm* the coroner and I say she's fine just where she is," her father said.

Holding up his hands, Ben protested, "Hey, man, I'm on your side."

Her father blinked. "You're right. Sorry. This whole day's got me on edge. Do you think I could grab some coffee? Last time I was here you had a pot going in the break room."

"Sure, man, help yourself. But I think that coffee is the exact same pot from the last time you were here. The stuff is like tar."

"You don't mind if I leave you for a minute?" Patrick asked. "Do you, Cammie?"

Cameryn shook her head and told him it was fine; she wanted to look around before things started. Her father disappeared through one of the doors, and she found herself standing alone by the large metal sinks. Ben was by the body bag, taking notes, so she turned her attention to the instruments that had been placed on the counter. They were lined up so neatly they looked like the teeth of a comb. Surgical knives, autopsy saws, scissors, large syringes, and a row of needles had been precisely arranged next to a dozen small specimen containers that would hold bits of organs destined for the histology lab. These she remembered from her books. She remembered, too, the yellow buckets, receptacles where the organs would be placed after they were sectioned, and the large pruning shears that would be used to cut through both Rachel's ribs and breastbone. A dual blue light, used to locate trace evidence, had been set next to an unopened rape kit. The possibility that Rachel had been sexually assaulted made Cameryn sick to her stomach, so to distract herself she once again examined the forensic tools.

Solid, inanimate objects—those were what she wanted her mind to focus on. Her fingertips skimmed the handles of the utensils, cold to the touch and glittering in the green light. What was she doing here? Her father thought she was a forensic genius because she found a baggie in a telephone book, believed she had nerves of steel because the second time around she didn't puke at the sight of a decaying body. But she knew the truth. She was a high-school student who didn't know anything except what she'd found in books. A spasm of anxiety shot through her, and her throat went dry. And yet, her father believed in her. He needed her. And so did Rachel.

Ben was still busy with his vials, so she went over to the body bag. Gently, she put her hand onto Rachel's vinyl-encased shoulder and bent to where she imagined Rachel's ear to be. "I'm sorry," she whispered. "I'm so sorry this happened to you." Only the overhead lights hummed in reply.

And suddenly, Cameryn did know why she was here. She who didn't believe in psychics communing with the dead felt something—whether it was Rachel's spirit or her own determination, she couldn't tell, but in that instant Cameryn saw her purpose. If she could help find the killer, she would do it. She would do whatever she had to. And even though she didn't believe Rachel's soul was still bound in her body, Cameryn whispered that promise to Rachel, over and over again, until she felt Ben's hand on her shoulder, pulling her up.

"Sorry to bother you, but the dragon master's watching you. He won't like you touching the corpse unless he's in here."

"Where . . . ?"

"Observation window," Ben told her. "To your left."

She hadn't noticed the window before. It was small, only three by four feet, with a curtain that had been pushed aside. A man's face glowered at her through the glass. He was stocky, with heavy brows and a thick, bull-like neck;

the corners of his mouth were pulled into a deep frown. What scared her were his eyes—he stared at her, unflinching, as if daring her to breathe, as if he hated her without even knowing her. They burned at her for a moment before the curtain snapped shut.

"Oh, man," Ben groaned. "Here he comes. Hold on—this could get ugly."

Chapter Seven

"WHERE ARE JACOBS AND CROWLEY? Where's Mahoney? And what is this child doing in my autopsy suite?" Moore barked as he stepped inside the room.

"Mahoney's grabbing a cup of coffee and the other two are on their way," Ben answered. "This here is Cammie. She's Pat's kid."

Moore narrowed his eyes, seeming to stare through Cameryn instead of looking at her. "Is that so? How old are you—fifteen?"

"Almost eighteen." Cameryn had hoped to sound strong, but her voice seemed to hush on the last syllable.

Dr. Moore gave a snort and jerked his lapels until they snapped. He turned his steely gaze back to Ben. "And you let her in here? A seventeen-year-old?"

Ben nodded but said nothing.

"Why?" Moore tapped a finger against his skull. "What are you, Ben, *thick*? This is a sensitive case—a homicide. I can't afford some neophyte tainting the evidence!" He pointed at Cameryn, then hooked his thumb with a jerk. "You—out! Go play with your Barbies!"

"Hold on, Doctor."

Relief flooded through Cameryn as her father stepped into the room. In an instant he was beside her, and she felt his hand rest on her shoulder. Its pressure told her not to worry, that he would handle this, and Cameryn, who usually preferred to fight her own fights, was only too happy to let him.

"This is my new assistant," her father said evenly, although she knew him well enough to hear an edge. "She wants to be a forensic pathologist, so I hired her."

"No way, Mahoney," Moore said, shaking his head. "This is my game and we play by my rules. The kid goes."

Dr. Moore reminded Cameryn of a bulldog: His heavy jaw protruded, and the thick fold of his jowls moved on their own when he talked. His head seemed to rest right on his chest, as though it had been absorbed by his generous torso. A white lab coat, oversized to clear his belly, hung past his knees, and she could see the faded scrubs beneath. "Out!" he said again.

Her father's fingers tightened so much Cameryn winced. "Dad," she whispered, "he doesn't want me here."

"Do you want to stay?"

She nodded firmly.

"Then you'll stay."

Cameryn wasn't so sure. Moore squinted at her through pinprick eyes, weighing her value, judging her. It seemed as though she were back in grade school, waiting for Brittany Naylor to proclaim who was on her team and who was not. Cameryn was always picked second to last and she could remember the feelings: relieved that Claudia Wilcox was considered even less cool than she was, but horrified at being so close to out. Now Moore was doing it to her again. She'd been studied and found lacking. She wanted to pull away from her father, but his grip was iron.

"You'd better check your rule book, Dr. Moore," her father said coolly. "You'll find you work for *me*, which means I have the power to remove you from this autopsy. You bounce Cameryn, I'll call in Dr. Canfield from Montrose. We'll take her up there and he can do the honors. Your choice."

"My *choice*?" Moore sputtered. "May I remind you that I have the medical degree."

"And may I remind you the body belongs to me. Cameryn stays or we all go."

"That's preposterous!" Moore cried.

Her father was unfazed. "That's the way it is."

Moore turned abruptly and opened a cabinet door so hard it banged against the wall. He muttered something inaudible as Cameryn watched the bulge that was the back of his neck redden. She looked up at her father, and his eyes told her to wait; he knew what he was doing. Cameryn wasn't so sure.

For a moment they stood, watching his back, until Ben, as if to break the stalemate, stepped forward. *Leave him to me,* he seemed to say, after which he gave her a discreet wink. Clearing his throat, he said, "Uh, Dr. Moore? I hear a psychic dude's coming all the way up from Santa Fe, New Mexico, because he saw a murdered girl's spirit in his hotel room. He says it's *this* murdered girl."

"Stupid people believe stupid things," Moore said. He balled up his lab coat and thrust it in the cabinet and pulled out a pair of latex gloves. Whirling a glove between his hands made the glove inflate like a balloon; when he squeezed it, the fingers popped out. "I'm preparing to do this autopsy right now, Ben, *without* the assistance of an underage child. Mr. Mahoney seems to think otherwise. I expect you to back me up here."

Ben said, "The psychic claims this is another one of those Christopher killings."

Moore yanked the gloves onto his hands. He stepped into paper pants and knotted the drawstring under his belly. "Has a Christopher medal been found on this girl's body, Mahoney?"

Patrick shook his head and said, "No, but of course we haven't—"

"I didn't think so," Moore cut him off. "The fact that some psychic wants to capitalize on this tragedy is not my concern. How did the media find out about this case, anyway? I thought as coroner that you'd keep the matter quiet."

"I'm guessing it was the women who found the body. They talked about the show when we interviewed them, so they could have called the *Shadow of Death* people. However it happened doesn't matter now—the story's out."

Cameryn felt her father's tension as Moore turned back to the cabinet and pulled out a blue paper tunic with elastic at the end of the three-quarter-long sleeves. He slouched into it. He removed a white plastic apron, which he jerked over his head, then tied the strings behind him with a knot. The doctor was acting as though her father's threat to take the body meant nothing, but if Moore believed that, he didn't know Patrick Mahoney. Her father would wheel Rachel right out from beneath Moore's scalpel. She bit at her nail and watched the two of them, each apparently as stubborn as the other. How was this going to end?

Ben continued to speak to the doctor's back. "The psychic—I think his name is Diamond or Jewel or something—he's already been on CNN."

Yanking on a pair of booties, Moore puffed out the words, "And I should care because . . . ?"

"Because the guy says he's coming *here*, which means he'll be bringing all kinds of publicity with him. This case is going to go big."

This was news. Dr. Jewel was coming to Silverton. Cameryn glanced at her father to see if it registered with him, but he gave her the slightest shake of the head.

Now Ben was all smiles. "I *know* you don't want this misunderstanding between you and Pat to be part of the story. And I *know* you don't want Mr. Mahoney and his girl taking the decedent all the way up to Canfield in Montrose. People need to see the work we do down here, in Durango. I bet the trial will be on Court TV and everything."

Moore seemed to be thinking about this. "You really believe this case will go nationwide?" he asked.

Ben's head bobbed. "Absolutely. Cammie—she's all right. Let's get to work instead of standing around here arguing. We got us a killer to catch."

Carefully, Moore placed a blue paper cap on his head, tucking the gray strands of his hair underneath. "Well, you do have a point, Ben," said Moore. "Catching the killer is the most important thing. Perhaps I lost focus of that for a moment." He turned, and with a crisp nod, gave his tacit consent. "Well, Cameryn, I suppose if your father wants to expose you to the indignities of death, it's not my place to stop him."

"No," Cameryn answered. "I mean, yes, it's not." She

blushed at how stupid she sounded, but Moore didn't seem to notice.

"Hope you've got the stomach for this. I'm not going to change the way I run my ship for you. Either you can handle it or you walk. Are we all agreed?"

"Agreed," her father answered. "Cameryn, well, she sees things. I think she has a gift."

"We'll see," Moore snapped. His next orders flew at her like bullets from a gun. "Get in your scrubs—you'll find them in that first cabinet next to the sink. You need booties, gloves, plastic apron, and, depending on how tough you think you are, a mask for the smell. She hasn't decomped yet, but bowel content is always dicey. I don't want you throwing up on the decedent."

"I appreciate your cooperation, Dr. Moore," her father began, but Moore waved him off.

"Don't misinterpret me, Mahoney. As coroner you've got the right to assign this case to any pathologist you want. True enough. But once the autopsy starts it's my case and I'll see it through. If your kid screws up, she's gone."

"She won't screw up."

Cameryn wasn't so sure. With trembling hands she opened the stainless steel door. Inside she found the green scrubs neatly folded, clean, but obviously well used. Dr. Moore said, "You'll notice our scrubs are secondhand, courtesy of the surgeons on high. You want to be a forensic pathologist, Ms. Mahoney? Then here's your first lesson—get used to hand-me-downs. Everything gets sent to the basement, just like the dead."

Cameryn slipped the green booties over her shoes, pulled on her paper gown, tied her apron, then put on the latex gloves. Silently, Ben handed her a surgical hat that looked more like a paper shower cap, and she quickly shoved her hair into it as her father donned his apron. Even under his surgical mask she could tell he was smiling at her, happy that his strategy worked and Moore had let her stay. Ben winked at her again; this time Cameryn winked back.

"Ben, I need music. Today I think I will listen to something fitting for the occasion. I want you to put in"—Dr. Moore's eyes searched the ceiling—"*La Bohème.*"

Cameryn stood directly in front of the drawer Ben needed, so she scooted over to let him by.

"That man always has to play the music when he works," Ben muttered, "but I say put on something to lift the spirit instead of drag you down."

"What was that, Ben?" Dr. Moore asked.

"Nothing, I'm just looking for Puccini." Ben shuffled though a stack of CDs before pulling one out and popping the disc into a boom box set against the wall. His voice drifted back to its former conspirator tone. "I hate this vibrato-y stuff. If it were me, I'd put on a little *Moulin Rouge.*"

He pushed a button, and the strains of Italian whirled through the air like florid smoke.

"'This Sea of Red passage makes me shiver,'" Moore said over the body bag. "That's Marcello singing. 'I feel as if it were flowing right over me, droplet by droplet.'" He grabbed the tag and with an extravagant motion unzipped it. "How apropos."

At that moment the door swung opened and Sheriff Jacobs and Deputy Crowley stepped in, their feet still clad in street shoes, which squeaked on the tile. "About time you two showed up," Moore said.

"Sorry, Doc, I was talking to the Colorado Bureau of Investigation." Sheriff Jacobs wore the same placid expression he had whenever he worked. Like his deputy, Jacobs wore blue jeans and a regulation shirt and thick-soled shoes covered with a haze of dust. "Our little town's not used to murder," he went on, "so I'll take all the help I can get."

Sheriff Jacobs touched his fingers to the rim of his cap, which was emblazoned with a golden stitched-on sheriff's star. "Afternoon, Cameryn, Pat. Been a long time since we've been at a homicide autopsy," he said to her father. "I'm feeling rusty. How about you?"

"A bit," her father agreed.

"All the way down the mountain my deputy here told me what's what. Crowley's been to quite a few of these things."

Justin ducked his head. Then looking up, he smiled at her, and Cameryn looked away, making it a point to smooth her features so they would be as indecipherable as the Italian that welled overhead.

Resetting his attention to include the rest of the people in the room, Justin asked, "Did we miss anything?"

"You missed my getting strong-armed into letting Cameryn in here," Dr. Moore grumbled. "Other than that, we're just beginning. You two going to suit up?"

"Just the paper gowns today," Jacobs replied. "Me and my new deputy'll take our pictures and sign the evidence bags."

Moore trained his small eyes onto the deputy. "So you're new, eh? It seems we have a lot of firsts today. Justin, is it? Do you know Cameryn?"

Justin nodded at Cameryn. "We've met."

"Ms. Mahoney's a newbie as well. You two novices should stick together."

Justin tilted his head as if considering. "That's Puccini playing, isn't it? Rodolfo's about to sing one of my favorite lines right . . . now." Closing his eyes, he recited, "'Love is like a fireplace which wastes too much.' That's good stuff."

Moore seemed pleased. "Ah, you know opera. Do you speak Italian?"

"Not really. My mother is Italian, though, and she kind of drilled this stuff into me. I can understand it okay, but I'm not fluent or anything."

So he knew Italian. She hadn't seen that one coming. While Cameryn pretended to straighten the seam on her paper scrubs, she stole a glance at him. Justin was shrugging on a paper smock. Then he and Jacobs stepped away from Rachel while Ben, her father, and Moore crowded around the body bag.

It was time, yet nobody moved. Dr. Moore waved his hand through the air. "Go ahead, Mahoney," he said, "the gang's all here. By all means, get started."

Her father cleared his throat. To the others in the room he looked confident, but Cameryn knew him well enough to tell he was nervous. "All right, Cammie, the first thing we do is move the deceased from the bag to the autopsy table. The second thing—and this is important—is we check the bag. There's probably nothing in it, but we search anyway, just to be sure."

"If the body was wrapped properly at the scene, then the bag should be clean," Moore interjected.

"The point is, no matter how careful you try to be, mistakes happen. Always check." Patrick aimed his comments directly at her, as if they were the only two people in the room. On the count of three, Ben, Cameryn, and her father pulled Rachel, still wrapped in the sheet, onto the perforated table, after which they examined the bag, which was empty. Cameryn felt her stomach turn as they unwrapped the sheet from Rachel's body. The skin on her nose, cheeks, and chin was rose-colored, like mottled sunburn, while the skin around her hairline remained ghostly white. Her nose had flattened. Bits of leaves were stuck in her hair, fragile as butterfly wings; a small twig was entangled in one of her locks. They pulled the rest of the sheet from under her and she lay prone on the table. With her hands beneath her back, the body rocked awkwardly, but her feet remained on pointe.

"The color on her face's from postmortem lividity," her father explained.

"I know—blood pools at the lowest point. It means she was put on her stomach right after he killed her." Cameryn kept her voice low.

Her father pulled a twist of hair from Rachel's face. The tongue protruded from Rachel's mouth like a turtle's head, dry and leathery. Eyes, now sunken, stared vacantly, as blank as stone. Although there was no smell, there was no mistaking the look of death, especially in those large, expressionless eyes. *Who did this to you?* Cameryn asked silently, but Rachel only stared in reply.

Suddenly Cameryn remembered a movie she'd seen, where the detective had been able to take a picture from the victim's eyes of the last thing she saw and place the image on a screen, and right then she would have given anything to be able to have that power. She moved closer, wanting to touch Rachel but at the same time wanting to recoil. Soon her fingers floated over Rachel's forearm until finally her fingertips drifted to the bare, freckled skin, cool and hard beneath Cameryn's latex gloves. *Why you?* she asked silently. *It could have been any of us in Silverton. It could have been me.* Bending closer, she saw her own pale reflection in the iris of Rachel's eye.

"Cammie!"

Cameryn snapped her head up. Her father had been speaking to her. "What?"

"Time for pictures."

"Yes. Of course."

The photographs began again, this time using a small L-shaped ruler Ben called an ABFO scale that he placed on various points on Rachel's body before shooting the pictures. Everyone seemed to have a camera—Sheriff Jacobs had his Polaroid, Cameryn her color digital, her father the black-and-white.

"ABFO stands for American Board of Forensic Odontology," her father translated. "It's so we can tell how large or small things are when we look at the images."

When they were done, Moore moved to the collection of trace evidence. "Watch how he works from head to foot," Patrick told her. "Everything has a method to it."

Dr. Moore frowned. "I suppose you're going to keep this running commentary going the entire time?"

Her father ignored him, but Cameryn found herself intrigued as she watched the pathologist's sure motions: First he ran a black, six-inch plastic comb through Rachel's hair and then folded the strands in a small piece of tissue paper. His strokes were gentler than she had expected, but still mechanical. Moore placed the tissue, plus the comb, in a paper coin envelope and handed it to her father. "Seal and sign," he said.

Ben held Rachel's head between his hands while Moore moved forceps over her scalp, his steel pincers yanking away tiny clumps of her hair first from the front, then from the back, finally from the nape of the neck. Once again he placed the strands on a tissue and dropped the folded sheet into a coin envelope. This, too, he passed to her father, who busily wrote Rachel's name, the date, the coroner case number, and the fact that it was collected by Dr. Moore. He then initialed the envelope and sealed the top with red evidence tape. That, too, was initialed.

"Now for the eyes," Moore said. He paused for a moment, his arm cocked, forceps poised in his hand like a conductor's baton. Music from *La Bohème* rose and fell in the background as he murmured, "My, she was a pretty girl, wasn't she?"

"Yeah, very pretty," Ben agreed. Ben's muscled body was planted solidly on the floor as if he grew there. His dark hands still cradled Rachel's head. "And way too young to die."

Moore sighed in agreement. Cameryn tried not to wince when the doctor plucked fifteen hairs from Rachel's left eyebrow. "Don't know why it's always the left side, but that's the way we do it," Moore said to no one in particular. "Here, Mahoney." He handed her father another coin envelope with the eyebrow hairs. "You know the drill—seal and sign. Now, let's see what we've got here. . . ." Pinching Rachel's lower eyelid with his forceps, he pulled it down toward her cheek, then pushed on Rachel's eyeball with a finger until the lower lid bulged out. The inside lid and white of the eye was stippled with deep red dots, as though bits of scarlet confetti had been sprinkled inside. "There's the petechial hemorrhaging. Usually, but not always, petechial hemorrhaging's a sign of strangulation. Cameryn, hand me that syringe there—no, the one with the short needle. That's right," he said when Cameryn had located it from a row of instruments. With a sure movement he jabbed the needle through the white of Rachel's eye and withdrew fluid, and Rachel's eye sank farther still. Something must have shown on Cameryn's face, because Dr. Moore said, "Don't worry, the mortuary'll fix her up again. Lots of times they rehydrate the eye to plump it back up. They just take a syringe of saline and . . . presto—instant eye." The vitreous fluid was placed into a tube with a red cap and then in one topped in gray. He handed the tubes to Patrick, who labeled them without a word.

One grim procedure followed another. Cameryn, her father, and Ben rolled the body on its side so Dr. Moore could cut off the tape binding her hands, which he placed into a large, inside-out Ziploc bag. He tacked down the tape at three points and then flipped the bag right-side out, sealed it, then dropped it into another, larger bag.

"Unfortunately," he said, "I've done this before. I've learned from past mistakes not to press the sticky side directly onto the plastic. The lab can never get it off. Criminals have a penchant for using duct tape, so . . . " He didn't finish his thought, and Cameryn didn't ask.

At every step there were more photographs, which she snapped woodenly. *We'll catch him,* she promised Rachel, over and over, one time for each click of the camera. *We'll get whoever did this to you.* Her promise sounded hollow, even to herself. Forensics had become cutting-edge, but there was still a cold, hard, statistical fact: Many murders, no matter how good the forensics, remained unsolved. Killers vanished every day. Cases went cold. *Not if I can help it,* she told herself fiercely.

Dr. Moore clipped Rachel's nails, folded them into a tissue, and dropped them into another coin envelope while Ben removed Rachel's four hoop earrings, each one laced with a small green bead. Seal and sign, seal and sign—over and over again the routine was followed. It was as if Rachel was a field to be harvested. In some ways the repetitive motion helped; every step was part of a script, every move preordained. But Cameryn couldn't help but notice how Rachel had ceased to be. Not just the fact that her soul was gone from her flesh, but the way her nobility as a human being had been taken. There was no dignity in death.

"Now we undress the victim," Dr. Moore announced.

Cameryn was unable to meet Dr. Moore's gaze. She was beginning to feel very uncomfortable.

"Every single item goes into a separate paper bag," he said. "Why do we use paper, Ms. Mahoney?"

"Because plastic can degrade the evidence?" She didn't mean for it to sound like a question, but it did. Still, she knew her answer was accurate and Moore nodded.

"Correct. Ah, listen to this part—it's Rodolfo singing. *'Ed i miei sogni usati, e i bei sogni miei, tosto son dileguar.'* 'Now all my past dreams, my beautiful dreams, have melted at once into thin air.' Ben, why don't you get Deputy Crowley there to help you. It's time for the new man to get his feet wet. You up to it, Crowley?"

"Yes, sir," Justin said.

"Good." Dr. Moore held out a scalpel and placed it along a row of instruments for later. It caught the light and cast a small reflection along the pale green wall.

Justin helped Ben push Rachel into a seated position while Cameryn unbuttoned Rachel's shirt. *It's no different from working in an emergency room,* she told herself. *Professional people get used to seeing the human body naked.* Now that Rachel's hands were free they dangled stiffly at her sides, and the two men struggled to pull the shirt off her wooden arms. Her father reached in to help, and soon the shirt was in a paper bag, sealed and signed.

"Now the bra," her father said.

Ben was reaching behind to unhook the clasp when a strange shape caught Cameryn's eye. "Wait!" she said.

There was a small, oval shape in the top of Rachel's right cup. The outline was tiny, no bigger than a dime. Reaching inside, Cameryn felt along Rachel's right breast.

"What is it?" her father asked.

"I don't know. I saw it and I didn't want whatever it is to drop onto the ground when we take her bra off. Hold on, I've got it. . . ."

With gloved fingers, Cameryn held up the small, pewter medal.

Saint Christopher, fingers raised in benediction, silently blessed her.

Chapter Eight

"OH, MY LORD, THE PSYCHIC was right." Ben breathed out the words as though he couldn't believe them himself.

"Well, well, well, what have we here? A medal of Saint Christopher, is it?" Dr. Moore clucked, leaning in close. He'd put on a pair of reading glasses, and the lenses winked in the fluorescent light. Shaking his head, he said, "Unbelievable."

Justin stared, wide-eyed, while Sheriff Jacobs made a feral sound in his throat. Her father pulled his chin back toward his neck and frowned. Cameryn slowly returned her gaze to the medal pinched between her gloved fingers. For a moment it seemed as though she couldn't move her eyes away from it, as if, by concentrating, she could make Saint Christopher open his tiny mouth and explain how he came to be in Rachel's lace-covered bra. The words SAINT CHRISTOPHER PROTECT US encircled an image of the saint, who, fording a stream, clutched a mighty staff in his hands. The saint's back was bent by the weight of the Christ child perched on his shoulders.

The medal cast off light like a pewter star, and Cameryn realized the scene in front of her made no sense. Here was the body, found beside a stream, the evidence of a serial killer, just as Dr. Jewel had said. But how could he have known? Her head roiled with thoughts she couldn't line up: her Catholic faith, which professed the power of medals but not clairvoyants, and her scientific training that reported only fact, the proof she held in her hand.

"Ms. Mahoney, you're holding a piece of evidence." Dr. Moor's sharp voice cut into her thoughts. "Put it in the envelope and get on with it."

"Oh, yes—I'm sorry." With shaking hands, Cameryn dropped the medal into the coin envelope her father had extended toward her.

"I have no idea," her father said, although Cameryn hadn't even asked the question.

"Any more medals in there?" Dr. Moore asked, pointing to the bra.

She could see no other bumps, so Cameryn shook her head no. "I can't believe we found it . . . just like Jewel said."

Dr. Moore's glasses had slipped farther down his thick nose, and he peered at Cameryn over the half-moon edges. "I realize a couple of you in this room have been thrown by this discovery, but finding the medal means nothing," he said. "Except perhaps your crazy psychic is the killer of this unfortunate child."

Justin cleared his throat. He crossed his arms over his chest, shaking his head slowly. "I already checked with the police in Santa Fe, and he's not our man. Dr. Jewel was the main event at the *Shadow of Death* conference down there—witnesses can vouch for him the whole time. It was the same in all the other Christopher killings where Jewel saw the victims. He's been at his conferences, on camera. He couldn't have been the killer."

"*Dr.* Jewel," Moore said, snorting. "Just what is he a 'doctor' of? All of those nut-jobs are bamboozlers and frauds—"

But the other men in the room weren't listening. "You called down to Santa Fe, Deputy?" Sheriff Jacobs broke in, obviously impressed.

"Yes, sir," Justin answered. "I checked around while you were with the Geller family."

"Have you ever actually seen Jewel's program, Justin?" Cameryn asked. "My friend loves it and swears he's for real, but I don't see how it could be."

"I've watched *Shadow of Death* before. Jewel has some amazing hits, but he's had some amazing misses, too.

When he's off, though, Jewel tells his audience that if there was a problem it's not because the spirits were wrong—it's because he didn't read their messages from the other side correctly."

"Balderdash," Moore said.

"Not necessarily," Justin retorted. "The police call on psychics every day. Dr. Jewel has proven himself with the Christopher killings and in other cases, too. I'm trying to keep an open mind."

"And I'm trying to get my job done," said Moore. He rapped his knuckles on the autopsy table like a teacher with a ruler. "All right, people, enough hocus-pocus. Let's get back to work." Raising his hands, Dr. Moore stood directly over Rachel, as if he were a priest preparing to consecrate the host.

"I'm going to help you out here, Ms. Mahoney. Now, as you can see, the victim's coming out of the rigor, which means her limbs are beginning to get more pliable. The rule of thumb is eight hours to get into rigor, eight hours in rigor, and then eight hours to get out of rigor, for a total of twenty-four hours. The victim's been dead—how long do you think, Pat?"

Her father rubbed the back of his neck. "I took a liver temp at the scene, which read about eighty-one degrees. A rough estimate would be that she died sometime around midnight, Saturday."

"So at this point she's been dead roughly forty-plus

hours. See," he said, picking up one of Rachel's arms and letting it drop to the table, "she's getting softer. But no matter what the state of decomposition it's always a challenge to get the underthings off. Watch me." With one hand Dr. Moore rolled the body on its side and with the other he deftly unsnapped the bra, removing it as casually as he would a piece of tissue from a gift bag. Cameryn winced to see her friend half-naked, to watch the galaxy of freckles exploding across her milky skin, but once again she reminded herself there was no privacy in death. Still, she was still embarrassed for her friend. From the corners of her eyes she glanced to see if anyone in the room reacted to the sight; they all seemed to respond to Rachel clinically, as though she were a specimen to be examined and no longer a person. Even Justin's face didn't register more than official interest.

"Bag it," Moore said, handing off the bra. "Shoes are next."

As they went on, Cameryn began to understand the rhythm of forensics. It became almost a dance set to its own music. Take pictures, remove a piece of clothing, bag it, seal and sign. The shoes, still bearing the checkerboard boxes Rachel had drawn with her ballpoint pen, were taken off, one to a bag, followed by the cotton athletic socks, the grass-stained jeans, and finally the pink thong with the candy hearts printed on the front. Dr. Moore placed a blue cloth over Rachel's hips while he worked, and Cameryn mentally thanked him, since no matter how many times she repeated that it was just medical procedure, the fact remained she was still the only female in the room while the shell of her friend was being stripped bare. When the rape kit was pulled out Cameryn turned away, suddenly interested in the row of instruments laid out on the steel cart. Justin, too, had turned his back. He lined up a row of head blocks that had been set out by the sink. He seemed intent on placing them up in a perfect row, so he nudged the end of one, then the other, like a child playing with blocks. A moment later his eyes caught hers. "You okay?" he mouthed.

Cameryn took a wavering breath. "Fine," she mouthed back.

Justin nodded.

"I don't see any sign of trauma," she heard Dr. Moore murmur as he swabbed Rachel's body, "although that in itself is puzzling. You'd think the perp would have wanted something more for his trouble."

Sheriff Jacobs leaned against the wall with one leg propped, stork-like, and answered him as though he were delivering a weather report. "The FBI told me none of the Christopher victims were raped. They haven't released that detail to the media, so keep it under your hat. It's been this guy's MO—kill and turn facedown, but no funny business."

At least she didn't have to suffer that, Cameryn thought.

At least he just killed her. But even that seemed empty, because Rachel was still dead. Dr. Moore squirted more fixative on a slide, and heard her father take it from him, still in the rhythm.

"All right, Ms. Mahoney, we're done with that part of the exam," Dr. Moore said, which let her know she hadn't fooled him at all. She drifted back to the table, to where Rachel lay white and bare and vulnerable.

Next, Dr. Moore fired up a blue light that he passed over Rachel's skin like a sapphire eye, looking, he said, for microscopic evidence. A pair of tweezers were poised in his other hand, ready to swoop and pluck. It was after one of the passes that Cameryn spotted it, although she wasn't sure if what she was seeing was real or not. She squinted and moved closer.

"Wait—go back—look at her hands," she said. "Dr. Moore, do you see it?"

"See what?" Dr. Moore asked. The light was still poised in the air, hovering. Cameryn could hear its faint hum.

She picked up Rachel's right hand and turned it, palm side up. "Move the blue light away," she said. "It's easier to see in regular light." It was hard to perceive since it was more of a shadow than anything, but Cameryn had seen Rachel's hands enough in life to know that this wasn't quite right. A faint cast, the color of root beer, had tinted the palm and fingers. It looked to her as though amber glass had been held over Rachel's palms so that a subtle reflection glazed the skin. Dr. Moore shoved his glasses up the bridge of his nose and squinted at Rachel's hand. "What are you talking about, Ms. Mahoney? I'm staring right at it and nothing's there."

"Yes, there is. Dad," Cameryn said, "do you see it? Look." She traced her fingertip lightly on Rachel's palm. "The color's off. It's barely off, but the skin's almost, I don't know, stained."

Her father bent close. "I'm afraid I don't see what you're looking at. The color seems the same to me."

"Maybe she put on one of those sunless tanning gels and forgot to wash her hands," Justin offered.

Cameryn looked at Rachel's body, prone and lily white except for the spray of freckles that scattered across her skin. "No, that can't be it," she answered, more to herself than to him. "There's no difference between her legs and her belly or anywhere else on her body. Look how pale she is. Besides, the color is just on her palms and the insides of her fingers." She bit her lip and looked up. "I think we should take a sample."

Dr. Moore was obviously annoyed. "Take a sample of what? There's nothing there."

"It's there," she told him.

"It's always the newbies who think they can see what a trained eye can't. Take a picture if you think you see something and then let's move on."

Ben shot Cameryn a warning look, but it was too

late, because she was too focused on the skin to word her response carefully. "I see it," she said. "Even if you don't."

There was a fire in Moore's eyes as he looked at her. "All those years in medical school for nothing when I could have known everything without studying, just like you. I lament my wasted life." Cameryn flushed, but kept her eyes on Rachel's palm. He watched her, impatient, while she snapped pictures of Rachel's hands. The second she was done he pushed past her and resumed scanning Rachel with the light, gliding it over her front before rolling her over to scan her back. He was pointedly not talking anymore, punishing her, Cameryn supposed, for speaking up. While the blue light passed over Rachel like a metal detector, Sheriff Jacobs and Justin shifted in the corner, sometimes watching, sometimes talking. Her father quietly checked the evidence bags. Finally Dr. Moore announced he was ready to begin cutting. "That is," he added, "if Ms. Mahoney gives me permission. May I proceed?" His eyes were hard as they examined her.

"I'm sorry if I sounded like a know-it-all. I didn't mean to, Dr. Moore."

"Think nothing of it. It's a pleasure to be instructed by a seventeen-year-old."

She opened her mouth to answer but Ben rushed in. "This is where it really gets interesting, Cammie, because the idea is to examine her from the inside out. You'll be amazed what Dr. Moore can discover just from going through the organs. He can tell what Rachel ate last and what kind of athlete she was and all kinds of things. You're going to learn a lot."

Dr. Moore picked up a scalpel while Ben turned on a hose Water began to flow into a large metal container perched on a cart next to Rachel's head.

"I'm sure this is redundant for Ms. Mahoney, but the first thing we do is the classic 'Y' incision," he began. Moore's scalpel gleamed as he cut into Rachel's left shoulder, then the right, in deep slices that met at the breastbone. With a whip-like motion he slashed Rachel all the way to her pubic bone as though he were gutting a fish. Even though Rachel was rail-thin, Cameryn still saw a half-inch layer of fat puffing from the incision like yellow insulation, and beneath that, muscle, meat-red and shiny. *This isn't Rachel—it's just what's left of her. Her soul is gone. This is only the shell.* Even though she repeated the mantra in her mind, Cameryn's nerves reacted on their own. Her throat tightened. Her feet wanted to move her away from the horror of it, yet she forced herself to stand and watch, focused and stoic. That was the deal she made with herself; agitation within, calm without. *This is only the shell,* she told herself again.

With a carpet cutter Moore severed sinew that held the

flesh to the ribs. Rachel's breasts disappeared as Dr. Moore peeled the rind of skin all the way to her sides, exposing the ribs like so many piano keys. "Cutters," he said.

Ben handed him pruning shears and Dr. Moore snapped off Rachel's breastplate, one rib at a time. He was breathing hard, and Cameryn wondered how old he was. The breastbone was pulled off and set aside. He reached into Rachel's frame and sliced again, pulling out her heart and handing it to Ben, who dipped it into the metal basin of water before handing it back to Dr. Moore. This time he had a bread knife in his hand. With a smooth motion he sliced Rachel's heart in two.

"Left ventricle, right ventricle," he intoned. "Looks normal." He placed it onto a terry-cloth towel and sliced again, flaying it a second time. "No clots or other abnormalities."

Standing inches from the open body, Cameryn could smell Rachel's blood mixed with a sweet hint of decay. But there was another smell, too, one that didn't belong. Puzzled, she bent closer and sniffed deeply, aware that Dr. Moore was watching her.

"Yes, Ms. Mahoney? You seem to have something to say."

Cameryn shook her head. "No," she answered. She was afraid to antagonize him any more than she already had, but her father looked at her, reading her face.

"What is it, Cammie?" he asked.

Her father was wearing a cap on his head just like the one she wore, only on him it had ridden back too far, making it look as though he wore a halo. She could tell the whole ordeal with Rachel had been hard on him. She could see the worry on his face. But his voice was so gentle she relented and said, "It's the smell."

Dr. Moore grunted. "This doesn't smell. You want smell? Try a corpse that's been in a plastic bag for a couple of weeks after it's turned to jelly. If you can't take this tiny bit of odor then you're pursuing the wrong line of work."

Cameryn shook her head. "No, that's not what I mean. It—Rachel—she smells like garlic. When I bent close to her lungs it hit me. It's there. I can smell it."

Dr. Moore leaned closer and sniffed. "So she ate garlic," he said. "So what? Do you want me to run a test for that, too?" Then, to Ben, "Do we have a test for garlic? Ms. Mahoney seems to think it's important."

"The point is Rachel didn't *eat* garlic," Cameryn said. "I know because she told me how much she hated it—she wouldn't even eat Caesar salad or spaghetti sauce or pizza. So it's strange that she should smell like something she detested. Am I allowed to tell you that, Dr. Moore? Am I even allowed to wonder?"

Her father's eyes widened. "Now, Cammie—" he said, but Cameryn held up her hands.

"I'm not trying to be rude, I'm just trying to explain

what I smelled. Why is having an opinion such an issue?"

She heard Ben suck in a big gulp of air, and his words from early morning rang in her ears: "dragon master." That's what Ben had called Dr. Moore, and she'd just challenged the dragon master himself. Dr. Moore just stared.

This time Cameryn thrust out her chin and stared right back, because she realized she had grown weary of pretending she didn't know how to think. Besides, it would take more than his snide comments to take her down—she'd been sparring with Mammaw for years, and her grandmother had trained her well. From the moment she'd met him the doctor had conveyed that he was in charge. He'd allowed Cameryn on board when he thought she would stand by and passively watch him steer. Now he glared at her as if, by speaking up, she'd committed mutiny. But she owed someone her allegiance, and it wasn't Moore. It was Rachel.

"I don't like your attitude, Ms. Mahoney," Moore said. His voice was ice. "You're a child who is in way over her head. Your naïve comments waste valuable time. You are a distraction—one I cannot afford."

"And with all due respect, you're not listening. There's something wrong here. I know Rachel. It's not right—it's something about this stain on her hands and the garlic smell. I can feel it!"

"So you're a psychic now, too. You and Dr. Jewel."

Cameryn flushed. "That's not fair!"

"You wouldn't even be here if your father hadn't forced the issue. But here's what's changed. I'm knee-deep in the procedure so this autopsy is now under my control exclusively. Watch yourself, Ms. Mahoney. I already told you once—I run a tight ship!"

"So you're not even going to check on the garlic."

"Garlic is not something our lab runs a screen for. Perhaps you can take a picture of the smell." He chuckled to himself.

It was that small laugh that undid her. The condescending, smug, dismissive snicker that said he didn't care what she thought, that she was young and female and therefore not to be taken seriously. She had done more than merely listen to him, and in that, he must have sensed a challenge. Her blood rocketed to her head and the words flew from her mouth unchecked.

"This isn't a ship and you're not a captain. You're a pathologist who should care more about the case than—!" She stopped herself then, but it was too late. The four of them—Ben, her father, Jacobs, and Deputy Crowley—stared at her, their mouths agape. Dr. Moore turned crimson, which soon deepened to purple. As much as Cameryn wanted to take the words back, she couldn't. The room vibrated with them.

"I'll ask you to leave," Moore told her, his voice low. "Now."

"Just a minute!" Patrick protested. "You can't throw her out! We've barely even started this thing. Cameryn's here with me and *I'm* not leaving—"

"I told you the rules from the get-go," Moore replied icily. "Your daughter is no longer a part of this."

Sheriff Jacobs asked where she would go for the next four-plus hours, but Moore just countered that it wasn't his problem—if the girl sat in the parking lot until nightfall then so be it; maybe next time she'd think before opening her mouth. Ben weighed in on her behalf as well, but Moore would have none of it. Cameryn stood in the midst of the uproar feeling miserable. Her father had trusted her to act professionally and she'd pushed too hard, said too much. Rachel lay on the table, half-opened, her still-wet organs shimmering in the light. *I'm sorry,* she told Rachel, her father, herself. They were stalemated: Dr. Moore insisting she leave, her father ordering her to stay, Cameryn caught between them. Then she saw Justin whisper something into Jacobs's ear, who in turn gave a terse nod.

"I'll take Cameryn," Justin said, stepping forward. A lock of dark hair had fallen in his eyes. He plowed his hand back though his hair, as though rinsing it in the shower. "I'm not really needed here and there's work to do at the station. Sheriff Jacobs can drive back with Mr. Mahoney when you get finished here."

The arguing stopped then and the room became silent,

as though it were taking a breath, while Puccini played on.

Her father began to protest, but Cameryn broke in. "No, I want to go, Dad. It's fine. I think I need to get out of here."

It was true, because suddenly she needed to breathe air that didn't smell like blood. Without waiting for a reply, Cameryn stripped off her paper smock and booties, still pristine despite everything that had been done to Rachel. Cameryn refused to look at Dr. Moore when he opened the door and gestured the two of them into the hallway. The door swung shut, silencing the music.

Cameryn looked up at Justin, whose blue-green eyes seemed lit from within. He leaned closer than he needed to, and Cameryn felt a blush creep across her face, as though his breath could somehow leave a visible trace upon her skin.

His voice was low. "Let's get out of here."

Chapter Nine

"I DON'T REALLY HAVE WORK to do in Silverton. I made that up," Justin told her as he pushed through the glass doors that led to the parking lot.

"Yeah, I figured that. Thanks for getting me out of there." When Cameryn stepped outside, she felt bright October sun on her face. Although it was cooler now, the white light stabbed her eyes, making her squint. It felt surreal, leaving Rachel behind. It seemed as though she herself had stepped from death to life, and the transition felt good.

"Over there," Justin said, leading her to the sheriff's Chevy Blazer. Two five-pointed stars had been decaled on the Blazer, one star on each front door, bright gold over the paint's sun-damaged silver. The car's finish reminded her of the polish on old coins, darkened from their journey through countless grimy hands. Justin opened the door for her and Cameryn slid inside.

He said, "You really gave Moore what-for in there, didn't you? I thought the old man was going to have a stroke when you told him he wasn't a real captain. Moore's an egomaniac."

"I'm surprised to hear you say that."

"Why?" he asked, cocking his head. "You don't think I bought into him, do you?"

"I thought you were a suck-up. I mean, with all that opera stuff? You were like a Hoover Deluxe." She smiled at him, her first, tenuous smile.

"Hey, that wasn't sucking up," he protested. "I happen to love opera. Do you want to stop for a bite to eat or something? Durango's a cool place and it might be good to take a break after all that."

Cameryn shook her head. "I just want to go home."

"Whatever you say."

He pulled out of the parking lot, turning onto Durango's Greene Street. Durango, too, was a tourist town, but it had done its transformation far better than Silverton. This town had fifty times as many stores, most upscale and expensive-looking with their striped awnings that capped the windows like medieval flags. Instead of trinkets, these shops offered top-of-the-line sports equipment next to stores boasting Hermès handbags. The real money stayed in Durango. If Dr. Jewel really was coming, she bet he'd want to stay here. Or did psychics even care about that sort of thing?

"What do you make of this Dr. Jewel?" she asked suddenly.

It took Justin a moment to answer. "Well, I think he's convincing. I can't see how the guy can be anything but real." He glanced at her, his eyes framing a question. "So where do you stand, Cameryn? Are you a believer?"

"I—it's hard to say. I would have said no yesterday, but today . . . I guess I need more information." That much was true. Jewel had almost proven beyond a shadow of a doubt that he'd seen the supernatural. Nothing fit in her world anymore.

"Man, you are a scientist at heart, aren't you?" Justin frowned. "I'm trying to remember—your people are Catholic, right?"

"What do you mean by 'my people'?" she asked, bristling.

Justin laughed at this. "Relax! My mom's Italian but I was raised Lutheran, and Lutherans don't have saints. I was just wondering about Saint Christopher. His medal had been left at every murder scene but I actually don't know much about the guy. Wasn't he demoted or something like that? If he's not a real saint what do you call him now—*Mr.* Christopher?"

"I don't know." The nuns had told Cameryn once, but the details were hazy, fogged over by disinterest and time.

"I think he was the patron saint for something but . . . I'll ask Mammaw. She knows all that stuff."

The Christopher medal brought her mind back to Rachel. Whoever killed her left the medal as a calling card, or perhaps a talisman, his own lucky charm to keep the police at bay. So far, it had worked. Rachel was the fourth victim. Four times in the last year the killer had strangled the life out of a girl and left her body in the wilderness. If they didn't capture the Christopher Killer now, there would most certainly be a fifth. The thought of yet another victim chilled her.

Moments later they were on Highway 550 on their way toward Silverton. Justin was a confident driver, and as he talked his hands lay loose on the wheel. Cameryn listened as he told her about his growing up in New York with his large family comprised of seven kids and various dogs and cats. "I love motorcycles," he said. "Six months ago I went solo to the Blue Ridge Mountains on my bike, and I'm telling you there's nothing better."

"So how did you end up in teeny tiny Silverton? I mean, how did you even *find* us?"

"Internet search. I went to the academy in New York, but I wasn't really that hot about staying in the city. Then I checked out jobs in the West. This seemed like a good place to get some experience, especially since I'm hooked on snowboarding."

She followed this with only half a brain because inside,

her mind churned. Thoughts of Rachel haunted her, and beneath that, Justin's comments about "the secret" hummed, like white noise. Still, as they drove, the knot inside her began to unwind. She let his cheerful words lull her away from the images of Rachel being filleted on the autopsy table.

"So what's your story? You got any other kids in your family?"

When she realized his question required a response, she shook herself. "Who, me?"

"Yeah. Who else?"

"I'm an only child."

"Your mom didn't want to give birth to a whole team like mine did?"

"Nope."

"My mom will have to call your mom. She'll probably give away a sibling or two of mine to even things out."

"I don't have a mother."

This seemed to surprise him. "Oh. I'm sorry to hear that. What happened?"

Sticking to her cover story, the one she'd told her friends for years, she said, "She died. And just so you know I don't want to talk about it."

"Dead. Wow." He sucked in a breath and blew it between his teeth. "That's too bad."

"It was a long time ago, so I'm okay with it."

He looked at her sideways. "You're seventeen, right?"

Cameryn nodded.

"How old were you when your mom died?"

"What part of 'I-don't-want-to-talk-about-it' do you not understand?"

"Sorry," he said. "I will say no more."

The trees of Durango whizzed by, tall clusters of pine broken by yawning meadows, and then they began to ascend the foothills that led up the San Juan Mountains. She put a foot up on the dashboard and let her head rest to one side. Justin chattered on, occasionally flashing a smile, keeping the conversation breezy. For one thing, he was amazed by the wildlife in Colorado.

"I mean, I'm from a place where a freakin' *dog* is considered exotic, and then I come here and *bam*—I get bears and cougars and all kinds of wild things. Case in point— look out the window to your right." Cameryn did and saw a herd of elk munching on stalks of wild grass, at least two hundred strong, strung out in a formation that stretched from one end of the field to the other. When she looked beyond the elk she saw the north side of the mountains, deep red, almost the color of blood. It was the same color that had pooled onto the autopsy table. She had to try to think through the evidence so she could stop the Christopher Killer. But where did Jewel fit in? Did he truly possess supernatural powers? If so, where did her faith, and her science, connect?

"Are you even listening to me?" Justin asked. "I feel like I'm talking to myself."

Cameryn's mind resurfaced. She looked at him and blinked.

"Man, I wish you could see your eyes—it's like you're here but you're not. You're starting to freak me out."

"Sorry. I was just thinking."

"About . . . ?"

"The autopsy. The murder. What it all means. By the way, did *you* see the color on Rachel's hand?"

"Yeah." Seeming to think better of it, he shook his head. "Well, not exactly. If I did it was barely there. But lividity can cause all sorts of funky things. It could have been due to that."

"Maybe," she agreed. "But the other strange thing was that I smelled garlic. What can cause a garlic smell in a person? I mean inside them, like in their blood? Do you know?"

"Besides the obvious, which is of course garlic itself, I can't think of a thing. I bet we could look it up, though. I've got some books back at my place. We could go there and see what we could find."

Cameryn noticed the change at once. *We.* He'd said the word "we" as if the two of them would work the case together. She was about to ask him what he meant by that when her cell phone sang the lyrical notes from *The Lord of the Rings*. It was Mammaw.

"Are you all right, girl?" was her grandmother's greeting. "Your dad told me you're coming back to town with the deputy. He's not very happy you're with the Crowley character, I can tell you that, so he asked me to make sure you're safe. Are you?"

Her eyes slid over to Justin. "Why wouldn't I be?" she asked.

"Just know your father doesn't trust the man. Watch yourself, is what I'm saying." Her grandmother's voice became tremulous. "But oh, I have to tell you my heart is breaking with the news of poor Rachel. It's a tragedy, it is, with the child dying at the hands of a devil." Even though it was over the phone, Cameryn swore she could hear her grandmother cross herself. "And I want you to know it's no shame, you leaving the autopsy because it was too much for you. You should never have been there in the first place."

"I left because Dr. Moore threw me out."

There was a pause on the line as Mammaw digested this. "Now why would he be doing a thing like that?"

"I'll explain later."

"When is it you think you'll be getting home?"

"Soon."

"Are you going to the store?"

Trying to keep the impatience from showing, she asked, "What do you need, Mammaw?"

"Don't snap—it's been a hard day for all the mothers in

our town." Her grandmother's voice trembled again, like a vibrato on a cello string. "One of our own is dead and gone. Rachel was too young, too young."

"Look, I need to go. I'll be there for dinner, okay? So . . . bye."

Cameryn didn't wait to hear if her grandmother answered. She wanted—no, *needed*—to think. There was something swimming beneath the surface that she couldn't quite see, clues she couldn't quite put together. If she could just concentrate, maybe she could get it. . . .

"So," Justin said, drumming his fingers against his steering wheel, "who's Mammaw?"

Sighing, she answered, "My grandmother."

"Father's mother or mother's mother?"

"Father's. She lives with us. Well, I guess I should say *we* live with *her*. It's her house."

"How long have you been with her?"

"Awhile."

"Not very specific, are we?"

"I already told you I don't want to talk about my family."

"You said you didn't want to talk about your *mother*. You didn't say your family."

"All right, I'm saying it now."

She twisted so she was facing him and noticed in the light the hairs on his arms were golden brown instead of black like the hair on his head. Sitting this close she could smell him, a mix of shampoo and aftershave that was probably supposed to suggest the outdoors but instead smelled musky.

Cameryn leaned closer. "Okay, it's my turn to ask a question," she told him.

"Great—fire away."

"Why does my dad hate you?" She asked this quickly. It was like a snap from a rubber band, and Justin flinched, almost imperceptibly. He pressed his lips together. His eyes were on the road, laserlike, and Cameryn realized he was not about to answer.

"Why does he hate you so much?" she pressed. "What did you do to him? Did you know him before you came to Silverton? Did you rob him? Are you his illegitimate child?"

"It's not my place to tell," he said at last. "Your pop made that much clear, anyway. I went to talk to him because I thought it was the right thing to do—I found out fast that I made a *big* mistake. But I'm not your brother if that's what you're thinking."

"I'm making it your place to tell."

"You can't do that. Look, Patrick set me straight a couple of days ago and you know what? Maybe he's right. I don't know anymore—this whole thing's crazy. I think I got in way over my head."

"Got in *what*?"

"Don't ask me to . . . Look, if you want answers, ask your family."

Frustrated, she blurted, "That's not good enough."

"It's gonna have to be," he replied.

A giant bug splattered against the windshield, a wet star in a dried constellation. Above her, mountains rose while the trees receded. Thready vegetation thinned until the peaks became completely bald. In some spots the rich iron ore turned the soil an orangey-red; Cameryn remembered that when she was little she'd thought the Silverton summit looked like the board of her Candy Land game.

"Those mountains are giant candy corns," she'd told her father years ago. She remembered she'd been small enough to be hoisted in his arms, and how she'd pointed to a splashing creek the color of caramel. "I want to taste some candy water." To which her father had replied, "Well, honey, things aren't always what they seem. You got to look way up the mountain to where the water comes from. See the waterfall up there?" He'd pointed to a powerful spray of water shooting off a cliff, and she saw the water was clear white, not orange. "It's not candy at all! Always look for the source."

Look for the source. A thought pricked her now, a connection as tenuous as the thinnest thread, one piece of information linked to another. All the beads slid onto it as she focused her whole mind on its pattern. Go to the source. Justin's source.

"What part of New York are you from? Originally, I mean?" she asked nonchalantly.

"Albany. It's a great place. But I moved to New York City after school."

She flipped down the visor and pretended to check her hair in the mirror. "How'd you afford to live there? I thought the city was really expensive."

"My oldest brother's a doctor so I moved in with him and helped take care of the kids. His wife's a doc, too. I just don't like to put 'nanny' on my résumé."

They had reached the summit and were now beginning their descent, winding down the mountain on a road so narrow it looked like a sliver of ribbon tossed on the mountainside. Below her, the cliff fell away into a sheer valley. Pines struggled to grow against gravity, stretching thin arms to the sun in worship while deep crevices, filled with granite rock, tumbled into the abyss like marbled water, more perfect than an artist's painting.

"There's an artist who lives in New York that goes by the name Hannah," she said, and then remembered the maiden name. "Hannah Peterson. She paints abstract flowers or something. Have you heard of her?"

He was silent now. A flush crept up his cheeks, spreading to his temples, and she knew then she'd scored a hit. When it came down to it, it wasn't really that difficult. There was only one subject she'd ever seen her father get angry about, and that was her mother, the person who'd disappeared into the art world of New York, the one who never called. It was that knowledge that had made the connection in her mind. She should have guessed it from the beginning. Once, she'd been on a Web site called "Six Degrees of Separation" and their ad said that any two people in the world can be connected in six steps, but she hadn't believed it. Now she did.

"So you know my mother." It was a statement instead of a question. "That's why my father hates you. You told my dad and he freaked out."

"I thought you said your mother was dead."

"She's dead to me," she said, feeling as cold as her words.

Justin tightened his jaw so hard his muscle twitched. "Man, you are smart."

"So they say. Why did you ask me about Hannah when you already knew the answers?"

"I just wanted to know what you really thought about her—what you'd say."

"How did you guys meet?"

He paused, then answered, "At a party at my brother's— he and my sister-in-law love to host big soirées with artists, musicians, writers. Anyone artsy. She was there and we started to talk. Hannah's a beautiful woman, Cameryn—she looks a lot like you. The two of us really hit it off. We spent some time together. She's pretty amazing."

Cameryn stared at him as his words ricocheted through her mind. "Oh my God." She could barely get out the words. "Oh my God! Were you *dating* my mother?

Because if you were dating Hannah, we are done! I mean it, Justin!" She sliced her hand through the air. "*Done!*"

"No—it was nothing like that," he stammered. "We were—*are*—just friends."

"You moved all the way out to Silverton to deliver a message for a *friend*? You've got to be kidding me!"

"Cameryn, listen to me—you've got it all wrong! I got this job in Silverton before I knew *anything*. Then I told Hannah where I was going and she freaked. That's when she told me about you—not before! I swear. You've got to believe me. Believe her—she *really* cares about you."

"Well I don't care about her."

His foot hit the brake, so hard that Cameryn felt herself pitch into the shoulder harness. Jerking the wheel, he pulled into an overlook, and the car, still running, shuddered. "Don't say that!"

For a moment she sat there, stunned. Was he *defending* Hannah? "You don't know what she did to me. She just *left*. And this is none of your business, Justin. *None of your business!*"

"Calm down. I think you need some air. Let's just get out of the car. . . ."

"No! I don't want to even think about Hannah today. You do realize your timing *sucks*!"

Suddenly, his voice was full of apology. "You're right, you're right," he said. "You're dealing with Rachel and it's way too much. I'm sorry. This isn't the way it was supposed to happen. I was going to bring you her letter and explain. She wanted me to *explain*."

"Explain what?" The hurt inside threatened to burst its dam, but Cameryn managed to say, "Explain why she abandoned me?"

He lifted his chin, and when he did the tiny sliver of scar shone in the light. "I think you should give her a chance. Don't judge her before you hear her story."

And then Cameryn did want out of the car because it felt as though she could no longer breathe. Jumping out, her feet crunched in gravel until she stopped at the edge of the overlook. She hugged herself hard. The mountain-side beneath her had been cut away, as sheer as a wall, and she felt the cool October breeze wrap around her like a shroud. Justin came up behind her but stood apart, unsure, it seemed, of what to do. Finally he spoke.

"You have to understand, Hannah had it all planned out. I was supposed to give you a present from her first. After you opened it, I was supposed to give you a letter. That's how it was supposed to go down."

Cameryn refused to look at him. In the distance she could see the mountain open up and the roads of Silverton stretch across the valley like a necklace. From her vantage point she could see the tiny houses dotting the grid of Silverton's unpaved streets. Solid, simple, and safe. She longed to be there, back at home, where her life made sense.

"So, what now?" he asked softly.

"I don't know. I don't know what to think anymore."

Although she hadn't meant it to, her answer seemed to encourage him. Justin took a step closer and she could see his shoes, scuffed and covered with dust, and the hem of his jeans breaking over knotted laces.

"The gift and the letter are back at my place," he said. "I'll give them to you as soon as we get to town. The point is your mother is ready to reconnect with you again. She wants to be in your life."

"*She* wants it? So now I'm supposed to pretend that it's all okay because *she's* ready? That's not how it works. Five years ago, maybe, but not today."

"Cameryn, don't—"

She faced him now, feeling her eyes going wide as she looked into his face. "Why didn't Hannah just mail the letter?"

"She thought you wouldn't get it—"

"Why didn't she call?"

"She said she tried—"

"Why didn't she come here *herself*?"

"Because she thought you'd reject her just like you're doing now."

"She rejected me first." And then the dam broke and she was crying, sobbing angrily, humiliated that she couldn't stop herself and more embarrassed when Justin tried to comfort her. She felt his hand lifting the hair from her face, but she jerked away, sobbing, "Don't! Just leave me alone. Please."

He pulled away, disappearing somewhere behind her, the car, maybe, or the woods. She didn't know and didn't care. Moving even closer to the outlook's edge, she stood and wept, and as she did time itself seemed to absorb into her misery. *Where is all this coming from, anyway?* she asked herself fiercely. It wasn't as if she hadn't known about Hannah. But before today everything had been kept neatly under wraps, and it had been better that way. Here, in the wild, there was no hiding from the reality of murder or resurrection. Life insisted on happening.

With her palms, Cameryn rubbed beneath her eyes, hard, gulping cool air. Justin had returned to the car and she could see him, looking down the road instead of at her. And then finally she joined him. Two cars roared past the outlook before he looked at her. "Where to?" he asked.

"Home."

The blinker clicked and soon they were back on the Million Dollar Highway. They drove the rest of the way in silence, past the visitors' center with its Victorian scrolled woodwork hanging from the rooftop like wooden eyelet, past the old-fashioned stores and the jelly bean-colored houses. When he pulled up to her house, she opened her car door before they had rolled to a complete stop. She was about to leave but, thinking better of it, she leaned back in to apologize. "I'm sorry, Justin," she said in a husky voice. "It's not you, it's Hannah. I'm sorry if I killed the messenger."

His green-blue eyes pierced through her. "Your mother still loves you," he said.

"I gotta go." Then, running as fast as she could, she opened the front door and disappeared into her grandmother's house.

Chapter Ten

THE SIDEWALK LEADING TO SCHOOL was cracked beneath Cameryn's feet, uneven rectangles of cement with gaps sprouting a few hardy weeds. It felt good to walk, to stretch her muscles and move her body, to feel she could at least physically go forward even if she was frozen mentally. Nothing had been settled in the past twenty-four hours. Not the issue of her mother (her father had stayed overnight in Durango, so she'd been unable to talk to him) and certainly not Rachel's death, the tragedy of which had triggered a media frenzy. Silverton was filling up with newspeople from as far away as California. Dr. Jewel himself was on the way. Trucks and vans had already rumbled into town, their tops bristling electronic spikes, their microphone cords coiling along Greene Street, snakelike. The Grand's restaurant was bustling, so much so that last night her boss had called her in to work.

"I'm sorry, I just can't," she'd told him, and he hadn't pressed. Then Lyric had called with the news that some Silverton residents, some of whom had never talked to Rachel in life, had suddenly become her best friends in death. "Everyone's lining up to be interviewed. The only one not running a freak show is Jewel—he's going to be here tomorrow! Did you hear he's staying at the Grand? Don't worry, he's going to find Rachel's killer. He was on the news, and he said this time the energy's really strong. Jewel will get whoever did this—wait and see."

Later that evening, Cameryn's Mammaw had come into her bedroom. Cameryn had been lying there, her pillow tight over her face so she could block out everything, until she'd felt the bedsprings sag under a new weight, felt strong fingers kneading her backbone, heard her grandmother's voice.

"You haven't said a word to me since you've been back and you've not eaten a thing. Was it seeing poor Rachel?"

Cameryn had nodded beneath her pillow. She wanted to be little again, before people left or died, when she believed mountains were made of candy. Surrounded by her own things and near her own grandmother, she pulled the pillow from her face. Mammaw, tied into a red gingham apron, smiled at her, her forehead knotted in concern.

"What's on your heart, girl? Tell me."

"I don't know if I can," she'd whispered.

"Try."

"It's . . . Hannah." She'd teared up but then forced them back. "What would happen if *I* had been the one who died? Could you . . . could you even find her? Do you even know where she is?"

Looking at her carefully, her mammaw had asked, "I don't suppose this sudden interest in your mother has anything to do with that new deputy, does it? Oh, don't look so surprised, girl. Patrick told me about his run-in with Deputy Crowley. I understand the boy's got a message from your mother that's he's dying to give you. Well, I don't like it but there's nothing for it. I've always told Patrick that secrets, especially family secrets, never stay buried forever." Her grandmother's fingers had spread across thick knees. "I know you'll be wanting answers, but I'm not the one to give them. You'll have to wait and talk to your father."

"Why wait?"

"Because," she'd said, "it's his story to tell."

Then, just this morning, when she hadn't been able to stomach her breakfast, Mammaw had tried again. She'd held her cup of coffee, handle side out, her blue veins winding on the backs of her hands like rivers on a map. "You've got to eat, girl. Starving yourself won't help. You've got to keep your mind alert."

"I'm not hungry."

She'd pointed at her with her cup. "It's been a hard time for you. But you must remember you're Irish, and we Irish know how to deal with life's blows. You've got to get back in the game, girl, just jump right back in the game," to which Cameryn had replied, "What if I don't want to play?"

As she made her way now along the sidewalk, a crack appeared, and Cameryn, remembering the old nursery rhyme, *Step on a crack and you break your mother's back*, planted her right foot squarely on it with as much force as she could. Nothing mattered. Cracks on sidewalks were just cracks. People died. Children were abandoned and mothers returned from limbo. Saint Christopher himself was just a calling card for a killer. When she'd prayed all those years for her mother to come back, it hadn't worked, and now that Cameryn didn't want her, Hannah materialized. There was no sense in any of it.

The early morning air was winter cool, so as Cameryn trudged toward Lyric's house she pinched the collar of her jacket tight in her hand. Up ahead she was surprised to see an old blue truck in her friend's driveway. A telltale plume of smoke rose from the driver's-side window. She registered the dark shape inside, slouching behind the wheel. Adam. Lyric was already outside, standing by the truck. She waved her over.

"You're late!" Lyric cried. "We've been waiting. Adam's

taking us to school today, okay? But come here quick, I want you to help me pick out my earrings."

Cameryn understood the subtext—they often did this when they wanted to have a conversation within a conversation. "Sure," she replied. She gave Adam a tacit nod and said, "Okay, Lyric, what are the choices?"

"Hoops or beads," she said. She was dressed in a flowered tiered skirt Cameryn guessed was a retread from the sixties, and instead of a coat she wore an oversized green poncho. Fawn-colored clogs encased her feet. Today Cameryn was dressed as usual, in jeans and a plain top. Her only jewelry was her Navajo flute-player earrings and a turquoise ring on her middle finger. She could feel Adam watching her, so she leaned close to Lyric and hissed, "What's Adam doing here?"

"I don't exactly know," she whispered back. "He called late last night—he's just absolutely devastated by Rachel's murder. He was really into her, you know? There's a lot of stuff going down in his life right now and I think he wants to talk about it. I mean—he was practically crying and then he asked if he could take me—us—to school so how could I say no?" She held out two pairs of earrings and said, "Which ones do you think go best?"

"Hoops." Cameryn pointed to circles the size of a bracelet. Then, under her breath, she said, "But I wanted to talk to you. I didn't even tell you what Justin said about my—"

"I know, I know, I want to hear, but we'll have to catch up later. We better go—he's looking at us and I don't want him to know we're talking about him." She dropped the beaded earrings into her backpack and slung it over her shoulder. There was nothing Cameryn could do but follow. Lyric huffed inside the cab and Cameryn squeezed into the remaining space, her right arm wedged against the door handle as she shut it. It was dirty inside, with a layer of dust on the dashboard and empty cans on the floor. Smears of dried paint were there, too, as though the interior had been finger-painted by a child.

"Is this your truck?" she asked Adam.

"My dad's. He's out of town." He flicked the cigarette out the window, then rolled it up. There were telltale smudges beneath his eyes. He looked as though he hadn't slept in days.

"What's going on, Adam?" Lyric asked.

Backing out of the driveway, he said, "There's bad stuff coming down. Really bad stuff. I don't know what to do."

"What are you talking about? You can tell us. Can't he, Cammie?"

Cameryn nodded halfheartedly.

Adam hesitated. "I don't know, man. There's no one I can go to but then I thought, maybe you."

"We're here," Lyric assured him. "Both of us."

He managed to say, very quietly, "It's my boss. He doesn't understand." Adam was driving beneath a scaffolding of branches, and the light that came through mottled his face. When he looked over he wore an expression that Cameryn had never seen before on him. He was afraid. Of what she didn't know, but the fear was real. The skull on the leather cord rolled against his chest as he drove and she began to get the uneasy feeling that she and Lyric shouldn't be there. But her friend seemed unfazed. Placing her hand on his forearm, Lyric asked, "So it has to do with your boss? What's up?"

"Yeah, okay, so as you know I like"—he swallowed—"*liked* Rachel."

Lyric nodded. "All of us did."

"I know, I know. But for me it was different. She was nice to me. She was real. So—my dad has this camera and I—the thing is, Mr. Melendez asked me to work on the yearbook staff and so I said okay. I took some pictures of Rachel. I mean, it doesn't hurt anybody to take their picture. It's just some pictures, right?"

"What are you saying?" Cameryn asked, not at all gently. "Did you take them without her knowing?"

He blanched. It took a moment for him to nod. "It wasn't bad or anything. It was just for the yearbook."

"This doesn't make any sense," Cameryn argued. "Rachel graduated last year."

Adam stopped at an intersection. "She came back to school one day, a couple of weeks ago, and ate lunch with a group of girls. So I took one of her laughing in the cafeteria with the others—I don't know their names. That's it, I swear. I'm an artist. I was using them to make a present but then she started giving me the brush-off. She wasn't really into me. I accepted that."

"So you put up some pictures of Rachel," Cameryn said. "I'm not tracking this. What does this have to do with your boss?"

"I have this darkroom in the basement of the souvenir shop. When I turn off my blue light there's, like, no light down there at all, so it's been perfect. Old man Andrews said I could use it. But I guess he went down there and last night when he found those photos hanging on the wall he lost it. He told me I was fired and he was going to report me to the sheriff."

"You had her pictures up? What, like in a shrine?" Cameryn cried.

Adam gunned the engine and pulled on to Greene. "*No!* It's not anything like that! I'm an artist. I was going to paint her portrait."

"Cammie!" Lyric said, shooting her a warning look. "Taking pictures isn't that big of a deal." She turned to Adam. "I think you're worried over nothing."

"Except it's *me* we're talking about." He hit the steering wheel with his hand. "Don't you think I know what people say? They call me a freak. Maybe I am, but I never hurt anybody. I'd *never* do that."

He drove past the school and pulled into the back lot, as far away from the other cars as he could get. Cameryn noticed that as he turned off the engine he was breathing hard. The bravado he'd worn like armor had shattered, exposing an Adam she'd never seen before, and somewhere inside she knew that he hadn't done anything to Rachel or anyone else. He was just a skinny kid hiding behind black clothes and a silver skull.

"Cameryn, would you please tell Adam that Rachel was the victim of the Christopher Killer and those victims were from places all over, like—like Virginia and I don't remember where-all. That means it *can't* be you, Adam. How could you have killed around the country like that? Am I right?"

Adam looked unconvinced.

Cameryn looked at her watch—five minutes until the first bell. She wanted to leave but it was obvious Lyric wanted to stay in the truck.

"You're giving in to the negative energy," Lyric said.

When Cameryn finally managed to catch Lyric's eyes, she pointed to her watch and mouthed, "I gotta go."

"You go on," she mouthed back.

Out loud she said, "I'll see you guys later."

Adam's head hung down, but he lifted it and looked at Cameryn gratefully. "Thanks. You're all right."

"See ya." She didn't return his sentiment. She wasn't at all sure she liked the thought of Adam creeping into their lives. And she wasn't completely sure she believed every-thing he said. Still, she didn't believe he was a killer. He was just weird.

She made her way to the front of the building. Ahead, she could tell the kids were abuzz with the story of Rachel because they swarmed the school steps, as though they were bees in a hive. Their heads were close together, their eyes darting. Usually, she slid into school unnoticed, but not today. The bees were waiting.

"Oh, look, there she is—hey, Cameryn!" Jessica, a waiflike girl from her class, waved to her. "Cameryn, you were at the autopsy, right? Was it gross?"

Cameryn didn't answer. Silverton students were like kids in schools everywhere, only smaller in number. Everyone had found their niche since grade school and stayed there like fossils cemented in their own rigid lay-ers. Cameryn, though, had always felt she could float through the striations, belonging to no particular order. The kids swarming her now, though, were the elite, and that was the one stratum she'd never felt entirely comfortable in. Neither, she knew, had Rachel.

"Sorry, guys," Cameryn told them, "I've got to run—I'm going to be late for biology."

Jessica thrust out a bony hip. "We were all her friends, Cameryn. You should tell us what happened. Everybody here knew Rachel. We all really care."

In a way it was true. The whole school had only a few

hundred kids divided among grades kindergarten through twelve, all housed in the same building. They all knew one another, which meant in a way they were a tight, if dysfunctional, family. Out of the sixty or so kids that made up the high school, seven were the kind who never talked to Cameryn unless they wanted something. Six of them were on the steps today, surrounding her now in a vibrating formation, eager to get some tidbit about the murder. She felt them close in around her, pulsating with curiosity.

"Come on, Cameryn, you were at the autopsy. Who do you think did it?"

"Like she'd know—the Christopher Killer could be anyone!"

"That's right—he might be from Silverton—"

"Or still be *in* Silverton!"

"Who says it's a man? It could be a woman. Ever heard of the lady who drowned her kids?"

"Don't be stupid," Jessica said. "Just ignore them, Cammie." Then Jessica put her hand on Cameryn's backpack and pushed her forward. The other kids parted obediently as the two of them made their way up the steps.

"I'm going to grief counseling after first period. I haven't been able to think of anything else—remember, Rachel and I shared a locker."

"That was in seventh grade."

Jessica's voice was dramatic. "But it hurts, you know?"

It saddened Cameryn to realize most of Rachel's true friends had already graduated. These weren't her real ones; they were just the curious kids who hadn't really known Rachel, the ones who were fishing for information so they could get on a television spot.

Jessica opened the door for her and the two of them stepped into the dim hallway. The air was musty, the way buildings smelled whenever they had been closed for any length of time, but it wasn't because it hadn't been used. It was because Silverton's ancient school was almost as old as the town. It possessed a gloom all its own, from dust clinging to the high foyer ceiling to the beveled windows that cast tiny rainbows against the walls.

Cameryn heard lockers slam down the hall, machine gun–like, and saw two smaller girls hurrying into the restroom. A knot of teachers eyed her, stopped talking, then dissolved into the front office.

Jessica kept the same intimate tone as they passed the drinking fountain. "Okay, now that we're alone I've got to ask. Are you going to be interviewed? 'Cause if you were, I could, like, go with you."

"I would never do that," Cameryn said.

"Okay, don't get so hostile, I was just trying to help. Things are going crazy, rumors are flying. Things in this town are just wild right now."

Her ears pricked. "What do you mean—what kind of rumors?"

"One says it's a trucker who makes a run from Durango to Ouray, and one says it's probably an ex-priest. Then there's a rumor that says the killer is that demented kid, Adam. I've been looking for him. We all have." Her eyes searched the hallway. "I wondered if he'd show up today but so far he's not here."

Cameryn's heart gave a frog-kick inside her ribs. "Why would anybody think it's Adam?"

"Why not? Everyone knows he's bizarre. And it's going around that his boss fired him. Anyway, listen, if you change your mind about the TV thing"—she crooked her thumb and her index finger and held them to her mouth and ear—"call me." Then she hurried off.

In a daze, Cameryn made her way to room 101 and slid onto her seat, a stool behind a counter lined with empty beakers. She tucked her feet behind the bottom rung. Had the story of the Adam's pictures of Rachel already been leaked? Gossip traveled like brushfire in a small town, so he might have been branded in the exact way he feared. But then, another more sinister thought worked in her mind, unsettling her. What if the rumor was right?

The majority of kids were already in their seats. Her science teacher was speaking to them, so Cameryn shook herself and tried to focus, but he was only repeating the same lines every adult said at a time like this—they were here to help and to come to any teacher or school official if they needed to, or knew anything. Mr. Ward was tall and thin, with short hair buzzed into a square that mirrored his square jaw. The final bell shrilled and Mr. Ward droned on.

Cameryn's mind kept drifting back to Adam. A sick feeling was spreading in the pit of her stomach. Had she been too quick to believe him when he declared his innocence? Worse, she'd left him alone in the truck with Lyric. Could her friend be in danger? Most of the time, those who knew serial killers would swear up and down that their friend could never have done it. One of the worst of them, John Wayne Gacy, had dressed up like a clown before brutally murdering over thirty young men. But Adam couldn't have gone all around the country, leaving new victims in his wake. Unless . . . A new thought jarred her. Adam could be a copycat killer.

A copycat. It was possible. The Christopher Killer had been in every magazine and paper for the last year. It wouldn't have been hard for Adam to read the details. Other thoughts worked in the corners of her mind, like spiders in the dark. Adam had a photo lab, which meant he worked with chemicals. Could something used in the process cause that faint stain she'd seen on Rachel's hands? Maybe there was a link there. Maybe, maybe, maybe.

She raised her hand. "Mr. Ward," she said. "I need to leave."

"Not yet, please. There's an announcement coming you should hear."

"But—"

The intercom crackled to life and the starchy voice of Mrs. Kellogg, their principal, filled the room.

"Good morning, students, teachers, and staff. I will be brief. As all of you undoubtedly know, we have lost one of our own. The memory of Rachel Geller will include all the good and generous things she has done, for her family, her school, and her community."

Mr. Ward listened, head bowed as if in prayer.

Cameryn glanced around the room again, and this time she noticed the other students, the girls hunched over, seemingly ready to cry while the boys stared ahead, their faces blank. Iggy, a large iguana kept in a glass aquarium, raised his head to the warming light. With one eye he seemed to stare at Cameryn; he blinked, then stretched his creped neck toward the manufactured sun. Beyond his tank sat a row of three computers hooked to the Internet.

Cameryn raised her hand again. "Mr. Ward?" she whispered loudly. "Could I at least go online really quick?" She had it in mind to check out the chemicals used to process film. But Mr. Ward shook his head no and held his finger to his lips.

" . . . because of the distressing nature of this occurrence, I have decided to dismiss school for the rest of the day, as well as tomorrow."

An eruption rose then, from her class and down the hall—cheering, clapping, and an occasional "Shut up, I'm trying to hear" from other students whose classroom door had been left open as well.

Finally the bell was rung, class was dismissed, and school, such as it was, was over. Hurrying out of the building, Cameryn rushed into the parking lot to the tucked-away spot Adam had parked the truck. It was still beneath a stand of pine trees in the corner lot, almost hidden by a brown Dumpster. Half-running, Cameryn went to the passenger side and knocked on the window.

"Oh my—you scared me stiff!" Lyric cried. "Don't sneak up like that—I almost had a coronary. What happened—did they call off school?"

Ignoring the question, Cameryn asked, "Are you okay?"

"Yeah." Lyric frowned. "Why wouldn't I be? Hurry, get in the truck. Adam and I were talking and I think I've got a plan. It's genius."

Adam still wore his haunted look, his skin paled to the point of translucence. "Lyric says it'll work," he said. "But I don't know."

"Of course it will work," Lyric said. "There's only one way to prove he's completely innocent, and that's to find out who's guilty. And I just realized the answer is at the Grand, right this very minute. See, Dr. Jewel has been talking with Rachel's spirit. I know how that kind of energy works. So does Adam. I think Rachel will talk to us and tell us who killed her."

Cameryn recoiled. "Oh, come *on!*"

"I got us in!" Lyric said, barely containing her excitement. "Tomorrow morning, first thing, we're going to *Shadow of Death* for a reading with Dr. Jewel."

Chapter Eleven

"I'M SORRY, KIDS, THE GRAND'S closed. No one's allowed in here unless they're with the show," a large man said, his arms folded across his thickly muscled chest. He wore a business suit with a silver nametag on his lapel that read PAUL PACHECO. Olive-complected, Paul had thinning black hair that had been combed straight back. His bull neck seemed to rise out of his shoulders, while his biceps strained against the suit's fabric, creating tiny accordion pleats and a gaping lapel. He stepped in front of the door to block it.

"But we're supposed to be in there!" Lyric protested. "I got clearance!"

"Yeah?" Paul thrust out his chin. "From who?"

"From Dr. Jewel. My mom, Daphne Larson, called yesterday and we've been invited to a private reading.

Go ask Dr. Jewel if you don't believe me!"

Paul's face relaxed. "Oh, yeah, yeah, Daphne—I met her earlier. Nice lady. You should've said something right off." Pressing into the door with his shoulder, he explained, "Half the town's trying to get in there and Jewel's not ready for the public. But you guys go right on in." With a small bow he swept the three of them inside.

"Wow," Cameryn breathed when she stepped inside the restaurant, "it's so different in here. George must have done this for the television show. I can't believe the transformation!"

It was no longer dim inside the Grand. Bright, incandescent light flooded every corner. Poles with lights on top lined the walls, like rows of giant sunflowers, and the air seemed to vibrate in their cast-off heat. Cameryn's boss had removed all the tables and reset the seats so that the front section of the restaurant had rows fifteen chairs deep and ten chairs wide, complete with an aisle planted right down the center. Beyond the chairs, Cameryn could see the back section of the restaurant, decked out like a talk-show set. Four plush chairs the color of plums had been dragged in from the hotel side of the Grand, and a table in the background bloomed with flowers so tall they seemed to fan the ceiling. Two huge cameras hunkered in the corners. A black woman paced back and forth, reviewing notes. Daphne was nowhere to be seen.

The black woman looked up and eyed them coolly. "Can I help you?"

"You—you're Stephanie Kinde, aren't you?" Lyric asked, obviously starstruck. "I watch your program all the time. Wow—you're a lot smaller in person than I thought you'd be!"

The woman was petite, reed-thin, and perfectly dressed, with her hair pulled back in a knot so tight her scalp gleamed like black silk. She wore a well-tailored navy suit with a crisp white blouse. A string of pearls encircled her neck and two more pearls dotted her small lobes. Chopstick hairpins had been stabbed through the bun, each pearl-tipped, and Cameryn thought they made her look as though she had some sort of antenna, perhaps to better channel the voices of the dead.

"Who are you?" the woman demanded.

Lyric flushed. "Uh, I'm Lyric Larson, and this is Cameryn Mahoney and Adam Stinson. We're here for a reading with Dr. Jewel."

The coolness vanished and the woman broke into a sudden smile. "Oh yes, you're with Daphne—she just stepped out for a moment to get some tea. Welcome to *Shadow of Death*," she said, extending her hand to Lyric, who pumped it enthusiastically, to Adam, and then to Cameryn, who felt Stephanie's nails dig into her palm, clawlike. "Please, have a seat and I'll let Dr. Jewel know you're here. You do understand that he's a very busy man and won't be able to talk too long. We're interviewing with NBC later today."

"Oh, we know that," Lyric said. "We just need to get in touch with Rachel's spirit."

"Then you've come to the right place," Stephanie answered. "Dr. Jewel has spoken to Rachel on several occasions since she first came to him in Santa Fe, and she has a lot to say about what happened to her. Later today we'll film a full show, but after speaking to your mother Dr. Jewel wanted to offer you a private reading. Would you mind if we filmed your session?"

"Film—like, in *film* you might use on your show?" Lyric gasped.

"Yes, as in our show. Of course, depending on what happens we may or may not use it. We just like to record the doctor's private readings. Our crew can set up quickly and you'll hardly know they're there. What do you say?"

"Absolutely!" Lyric, once again, answered for them all.

"Excellent. Wait here and I'll be right back." With that, Stephanie turned on a stiletto heel and disappeared though the door that connected the restaurant to the Grand Hotel.

Adam bit his lip nervously. "You didn't tell anyone we were coming here, did you?" he asked.

"No," Lyric replied. "Just my mom. I had to because she's the one who could get us in here."

"What about you, Cameryn?"

"I didn't tell anyone, either." There was no way Cameryn wanted to admit to anyone she was here. Once again delayed, her father was scheduled to come home that afternoon, and the two of them had more important issues to deal with than psychics. If her mammaw knew, she'd just give her grief. No, Cameryn had thought it best to keep this under wraps.

Adam looked relived. "Good," he said.

It was then that Cameryn realized he had on the same outfit he'd worn yesterday. His hair looked grimy and unwashed, his clothes seemed rumpled. "You haven't been home, have you?" Cameryn asked.

"I swung home quick and grabbed a sleeping bag and some food, and then I stayed in my truck. I figure the sheriff has to find me to arrest me."

"I already told you, Sheriff Jacobs won't arrest you for having pictures." *Or anything else*, she silently added. Last night she'd been busy on her own Internet search, looking up chemicals used in processing film. She'd discovered silver halide crystals, hydroquinone, catechols, and aminophenols, none of which produced either a brown tint on the skin or a garlic smell. It relieved her to find no links between Adam and the murder, but still, she felt wary of him. And that feeling extended beyond Adam—she was also extremely skeptical of any so-called "help" Dr. Jewel could provide. But everyone else was a believer. This morning she was very much the odd girl out.

"So, isn't this exciting?" Lyric asked. "If you ever watched *Shadow of Death*, Cammie, you'd realize Stephanie's a real psychic, too. She helps Dr. Jewel on his show."

"It she's a real psychic then why did we have to introduce ourselves?" Cameryn quipped, unwilling to get sucked in.

"I don't know." Narrowing her eyes, Lyric said, "Don't start, okay?"

"I'm just saying that if Stephanie was a true psychic then she should have *known* you were Lyric and I was Cameryn."

"You're not going to be so cynical when Dr. Jewel arrives, are you?" a voice from behind her asked. Turning, Cameryn looked directly into Daphne Larson's smiling face. "Darling," she said, "you must remember that psychic energy is drained away by unbelief. You've always been such a closed shell. You've got to open your mind, Cammie. We can't have your negativity affecting the reading."

Daphne was an older version of her daughter. A heavy woman with fleshy arms, Lyric's mother had encased herself in a tie-dyed blue-and-green muumuu that reached all the way to her sandals, which she wore year-round. Brightly colored beads cascaded down her chest like a waterfall, and her hair, long and white, curled wildly to the middle of her back. Although Cameryn didn't believe half of what Daphne said, she liked her. She always made Cameryn feel welcome, freely offering her an abundance of natural food from her kitchen, including piles of cookies made from honey and raw milk and steaming mugs of herbal tea. Daphne insisted on being called by her first name because she claimed age should never be a barrier to friendship. "You may be young in years, Cameryn," Daphne often told her, "but you're an old soul."

"Don't worry, Daphne," Cameryn assured her now, "I'll behave myself. I promise. I know if it weren't for you, we wouldn't even be here."

"I'm glad you appreciate that. I've contributed to Jewel for years, and when I told them we needed help, the *Shadow of Death* crew was right there. His private readings are normally booked years in advance."

Stephanie reappeared then with release forms to sign, which the three of them did. A couple of ponytailed cameramen rolled out cameras and positioned themselves. Stephanie directed Cameryn to the audience chairs, Adam and Lyric to the stage chairs. More lights were pointed on Adam, who looked nervous, and Lyric, who seemed ready to burst with excitement. A moment later, Daphne joined Cameryn in the audience, which left her two friends staring at the cameras, anxious and expectant.

"You guys ready?" Stephanie asked.

"Absolutely!" Lyric replied.

Adam didn't look as sure, but he nodded. His eyes, still lined with smudges of kohl, seemed too large in his face. "Yeah. Yeah, I'm ready."

Stephanie became all-business. "What's going to happen now is we're going to film this like we would a regular taping of *Shadow of Death*." Without breaking eye contact, she made a slight motion with her hand. A plump woman in a smock hurried to where they stood and began to powder Adam's face.

"As you know," Stephanie went on, "some of our shows are broadcast live, particularly after a conference like the one we had in Santa Fe. In that case we wanted to help the police find Rachel's remains as quickly as possible. Most shows, however, are taped. That's what will happen here. Remember, we may or may not use any of what we're going to film now—that all depends on how compelling the reading is. So, on your part, try to pay attention and stay open to the messages from beyond."

"What do you mean?" Adam asked. Then, to the make-up woman, he whispered, *"Stop!"*

"I mean when Dr. Jewel says something that makes sense to you, for heaven's sake, *acknowledge* him." She pursed her lips. "In terms of a show, there's nothing worse than doing a reading on nonresponsive people. Can you show enthusiasm?"

"I watch *Shadow of Death* all the time and I know

exactly what to do," said Lyric, who eagerly turned her face to the makeup woman's brush. "I'm ready."

Stephanie smiled. "Good." She smoothed her skirt and turned to the closest camera while one of the ponytailed men behind it counted down on his fingers. When he got to only one, Stephanie's smooth features lit up. "Welcome to a private meeting with world-renowned psychic, paranormal expert, and spiritualist, *Dr. Raymond Jewel!*"

Daphne pumped her hands together so hard her fleshy arms jiggled in waves. To Cameryn she whispered, "Whether you believe it or not, Dr. Jewel's the real deal. Watch and learn."

And then, to the side, a door swung open, and Dr. Jewel swept into the room. Like Stephanie, he was shorter than he appeared on TV. Jewel's face was handsome even though his too-tanned skin had turned the color of saddle leather. Steel-gray hair, combed straight back, hung past the collar of some sort of tunic, and he wore jeans and moccasins with beaded flaps. He looked like an old hippie, only the kind with money. One detail of his appearance shouted Hollywood: When he smiled, his teeth were too white and square, like the row of bleached tile behind her grandmother's sink. He must have paid a lot for that smile.

"Lyric, Adam, welcome to *Shadow of Death,*" Jewel said, open-armed. He leaned in and air-kissed Lyric, once on each cheek, gripped Adam's hand hard enough to make him wince, and then graciously acknowledged his audience of two. He had a performer's voice. Despite Cameryn's vow to keep an open mind, her first impression was that she didn't like the man. Perhaps he had the power to read her thoughts because from that moment on he ignored her.

Dropping into a chair, he trained his professional gaze onto Lyric. "Tell me about yourself," he asked softly. "I'm listening."

"Uh, what do you want me to say?" Lyric asked.

"Whatever comes to your mind." He was smiling, relaxed. "There's no right or wrong here. I just want to get a bead on your energy."

For the next fifteen minutes, Dr. Jewel went from Lyric to Adam to Lyric again, probing them, and Cameryn guessed he was making mental notes, gaining their confidence. As they answered he watched them with keen eyes. Finally he said, "We've had a good visit here, but I think it's time we move on. We're going to begin taping now." He signaled to the cameramen and the red lights of the cameras blinked on. "So, why don't you tell me why you're here. Who do you want to contact on the other side?"

Lyric, as usual, was the first to answer. "I'm—we're here to reach Rachel, the Silverton girl who got killed. Murdered. She was a friend of mine. Of *ours*." Cameryn could tell Lyric was nervous because her voice was unnaturally high, as if she'd taken a hit of helium.

"And why do you want to speak to her?"

"Because I want to see if she'll tell you who the real killer is. An innocent person might be accused and I want to help him. I know he didn't do it." She looked at Adam, then back to Jewel. "If you lead the police to the real killer, then my friend will be off the hook. It's really important that you help us find the real killer."

"I see you have a compassionate heart," Jewel said.

Lyric blushed. "Thank you. You've talked to Rachel before, right? She appeared to you in Santa Fe."

"Yes, Rachel has spoken to me. And I can tell you that Rachel is safely over on the other side. She's in the light. Your friend has crossed through the shadow of death."

"I knew she'd made it," Lyric exclaimed. "Will she mind coming back? Can you contact her now?"

"I can try. Of course you realize my gift doesn't allow me to just place an order and have the correct spirit appear. I can ask for Rachel, but other energies are usually trying to get through as well." Then he trained his eyes on Adam. "But before I try, I have an impression about you. I don't mean to be offensive, but—are you the friend who is in trouble?"

This surprised Cameryn, until she realized Daphne had probably given Jewel the details. Leaning close, she whispered, "Did you tell Jewel about Adam?"

"No," Daphne retorted. "I didn't say a word."

"Then how could he . . . ?"

"Because he's a psychic. Hush, now, I'm trying to hear."

Adam had nodded agreement, which Jewel seemed to accept without judgment or surprise. Cameryn wrinkled her brow, trying to figure it out. The science side of her said Jewel had no inside track to the beyond. The spiritual side—the part of her that believed in the unseen—reminded her Jewel had already discerned a key piece of information in Rachel's murder. And now it was unnerving to have him finger Adam so quickly. But then she reminded herself of the other bit of information she'd discovered on the Internet: How psychics could fake it. In fact, many were masters of the fake-out. She certainly hadn't become an expert overnight, but she was aware of the ways psychics could pull information from their clients. They even had names for the strategies: the Russian Doll, the Fuzzy Facts, the Lucky Guess, the Sugar Lump—all of those and more were ways they got clients to reveal themselves.

"Isn't he amazing?" Daphne asked.

"He is. But Lyric kind of told him it was Adam."

Daphne looked at her, incredulous. "What are you talking about?"

Cameryn whispered, "Lyric said 'an innocent person has been accused and I want to help *him*.' That let Jewel know the accused person was a male. And then she looked at Adam."

Daphne sighed. "Cynic," she said.

"Can you help him?" Lyric was asking now. The earrings she'd discarded yesterday now dangled to the tips of her shoulders, quivering with her every word.

"I'm trying. Let me see if she'll come through." Jewel's lids fluttered shut. And then, nothing. Cameryn shifted uncomfortably as she waited, until in a hushed voice she said, "I don't think it's working," to which Daphne whispered, "Rachel's crossing over—it takes time. Just wait."

Finally, Jewel's eyes drifted open, and he eyed the camera dreamily. "Yes, she's here. I don't know what this means, but she's telling me about the color blue. Does the color blue mean anything to you, Lyric?"

Daphne leaned forward in her seat, entranced, her beads spilling onto her knees. Cameryn watched Adam's eyes widen. "Wait," he said, "you're saying that Rachel's here, in this room? Right now? In the Grand?"

A look of amusement played at the corners of Jewel's lips. "Yes, Adam. Rachel's standing right behind you, actually."

The cameramen followed Adam as he whipped around in his seat. Apparently seeing nothing, Adam turned back to Jewel. Then, with one more quick glance over his shoulder, he asked, "You're *sure* she's standing there?"

"Oh, yes, I see her. She's a very beautiful girl," Dr. Jewel said. "I see long, brown hair and a pretty smile. But I think her hair was actually red before she colored it. On the other side, her hair changes from red to brown, like flashes of light."

Once again, Cameryn was startled. How would he know about Rachel's hair? That was more than a lucky guess—Rachel had dyed her hair for years. Did Jewel somehow gain access to the coroner files?

"She's holding up a watch with no hands," Jewel said now. "The clock tells me she wasn't ready to die. Now she's extending a white rose, which means she's accepted it and is in her bliss." His eyes fluttered again. "Rachel's holding up her hand for me and I can see she's wearing jewelry . . ." Now Jewel squinted. "It's a bracelet, I think. And earrings. Hoops, I believe. Are those blue beads on them?" he asked the air. Then, shaking his head, he corrected himself. "I'm sorry. They are green."

Cameryn felt her whole body react. *How could he have known about the earrings?*

"Rachel's trying to let you know she's really here, so allow the validation. She's made her way here, and she's telling me she's anxious to talk. So let's get back to the color blue. What does blue mean? And the letter *M*? This can go to either one of you, please? I'm listening."

Lyric stared blankly, and Adam shrugged his shoulders.

"All right, we'll set it aside, but I want you to remember what I said. When you look back I know you'll discover a connection to that color. Again, Rachel wants to validate that it's her coming through. Now, besides blue and the *M* there's the number eight. What does the number eight mean to you?" Jewel seemed to be warming up—his words were coming more rapid-fire now. "It could be a date, or an address, or her locker number—"

"Her locker number was thirty-*eight*!" Lyric said.

"No, that's not it." Jewel shook his head hard, but his hair stayed in place. Stephanie had eased into the chair next to him, and she, too, was concentrating on the space behind Adam.

"I'm getting the same number you are," Stephanie told Jewel. "It's something specific to the number eight. Adam, does the number eight make sense to you?"

"No."

"Me neither," Lyric said.

"Actually, I'm getting even more. I think it's an eight and then another eight. Eighty-eight. Does that mean anything to either one of you?"

"No. I'm sorry," Lyric replied. "Are you getting anything, Adam?"

"Nothing. But I don't care about blue or the number eight—can you ask her who killed her?" Adam blurted out. "Can she tell us his name?"

Stephanie, who had taken a chair next to Jewel, looked concerned. "What is it, Doctor?"

Jewel pressed his fingertips into his forehead. "It's hard

for those who have passed to talk about their deaths, especially when their passing was violent. I can feel her distress. She's trying to show me something. It's a male or female figure, close to the same age as Rachel because she's pointing to her right side, which means someone in her space continuum, in other words, someone *like* her, in and around her age range. I believe she wants to tell us her killer was someone close to her age."

"Someone close to her age?" Lyric repeated.

"Why is Rachel shaking her head and pointing to her neck, please? I'm listening." As suddenly as the sun dipped behind a cloud, the man's face darkened. "Was she strangled, please? Rachel's indicating to me that there was a pressure. Yes, a terrible pressure right . . . here." He pointed to his own Adam's apple. "She's telling me she had the air pressed out of her. And pain. She's saying she wasn't ready. She's telling me she couldn't breathe. . . . Does this make sense to either one of you? Please"—Jewel almost choked on words—"I'm listening."

And then, before anyone could answer, Paul Pacheco's voice boomed from the front of the Grand. "Hey, Dr. Jewel's giving a private reading—they're taping in there. No one interrupts a taping," followed by a response Cameryn couldn't make out, and then, "Come on, can't this wait until the doc's done?"

"Sorry," came the reply, louder this time. "This is police

business." Cameryn immediately recognized the voice of Sheriff Jacobs.

"Oh, no," Daphne moaned, "you can't stop a reading right in the middle—Rachel might leave!"

Twisting in her seat, Cameryn tried to take in what was happening. Justin and Sheriff Jacobs appeared at the back of the room, followed by Paul, his thick neck bulging with frustration as he hurried behind them.

Paul looked worried. "I'm sorry, Dr. Jewel," he cried, lifting his hands in the air. "I tried but I couldn't stop them."

"Keep those cameras rolling," Jewel ordered quietly. Then he said, "It's not a problem, Paul. Go back to your post." Next he addressed Sheriff Jacobs. "I'm here to help you in any way I can. What is it you want?"

"I'm sorry to interrupt, but we need to speak with Adam," Jacobs answered. He planted his feet squarely on the wooden floor and stood unmoving. Justin did the same. Cameryn tried to catch Justin's eye so she could better read what was going on, but he didn't look at her. He kept his eyes fixed on Adam.

Jewel said, "Perhaps you don't realize we're in the middle of a reading."

"I can see that," Jacob's answered. "But this can't wait."

Dr. Jewel stiffened. "That's a pity. Rachel's here, right now, you see. You can talk with her if you like. I work with the police all the time and my ability to speak with the dead has cracked many a case. Perhaps you have a few questions you'd like to ask Rachel yourself."

"Not today," Sheriff Jacobs told him. He walked to the stage area, stopping directly in front of Adam, who looked up at him with scared eyes. "Son," Jacobs said, "you need to come with me."

The cameras rolled on. Each cameraman had a lens trained on Jewel, on his face. Adam reached over to grip Lyric's hand, and it seemed to Cameryn as if the whole room held its breath.

In a broken voice, Adam asked, "Is this because of the pictures?"

Jacobs looked surprised. "I'm not here because of any pictures, although I'd be mighty interested to hear about them now."

Confused, Adam said, "Then . . . why?"

"I'm here because there was a witness who saw you leave the Grand with Rachel. That witness also states he saw you helping her into your truck. That means you were the last one to see that girl alive."

"That's not true!" Lyric exploded. "Adam, tell him it's not true!"

But when Cameryn looked into Adam's face, she knew it *was* true. And just as quickly, Lyric did, too. She jerked her hand from his as though it were on fire.

"It's—it's not what it sounds like," Adam stammered. "I was afraid to tell you. Lyric, I *swear* I didn't do this."

"That's enough, son. We'll do the rest of the talking in

my office." Sheriff Jacobs pulled Adam to his feet and began to read him his Miranda rights. Adam stood, frozen, his fists clenched so tight the skin on his knuckles blanched white. When Jacobs had finished, he placed his hand on Adam's shoulder. "It's just for questioning," he told him. "Don't make it harder than it needs to be."

"You believe me, don't you, Lyric?" Adam asked hoarsely. "You know I couldn't hurt Rachel. I wouldn't hurt anyone! Ask her. Make Dr. Jewel ask Rachel herself. She'll tell you!" He had turned to face Lyric, but she refused to return his gaze. It was then that Adam seemed to collapse in on himself. Without another word he slumped between the sheriff and Justin as they escorted him out of the Grand. The room became suddenly still. Dr. Jewel lowered his head, holding it between his fingertips.

"What is it, Doctor?" Stephanie finally asked, her voice hushed. "What's wrong?"

Jewel shook his head slowly from side to side. "He's right. It's not the boy. I'm telling you, he's not the one."

"Are you sure?" Stephanie gasped.

"Yes. Rachel's holding up a Christopher medal and placing it on her heart, then holding the letter *A*." To the camera he said, "But she's saying no. She's saying no to Adam."

Stephanie murmured, "I don't understand."

Suddenly Jewel covered his eyes; no muscles moved except those in his mouth. "Rachel is telling me the killer is still out there."

"Still out there?"

"Yes. He's here, in Silverton. And Rachel says . . ." Jewel's voice quavered. Even from a distance Cameryn could see him tremble. "She says . . . the real Christopher Killer is ready to strike again."

Chapter Twelve

"YOU SHOULD NEVER HAVE GONE to the Grand," Mammaw scolded. "If you were wanting to talk to poor Rachel then you should've gone to church, lit a candle, and sent up a couple prayers. And I'll tell you something else," she said, leveling a spatula at Cameryn. "If Dr. Jewel puts that interview on television it could ruin Adam's life. The public will forever find the boy guilty, trial or no."

"Dr. Jewel says he's going to air it the day after tomorrow," Cameryn answered. With her head down, her hair fell forward, and she felt like hiding inside it. She'd been home from the Grand less than an hour. As she peeked at her grandmother from the slender part in her hair, she said, "That's the day of Rachel's funeral."

"The man's trying to make money off of others' misery," her grandmother told her. Her own hair had been pulled back into a knot at the nape of her neck. A few loose strands had escaped, curling up like springs. Scooping a blob of chocolate frosting, Mammaw plopped a mound onto the top of the cake. "Well, it's all nonsense and no educated person'll believe any of it." Her grandmother pursed her lips. "The very idea that Dr. Jewel is channeling poor Rachel's spirit!" She made a *tsk*ing sound between her teeth as she scraped at the ceramic bowl.

"I don't think he's actually channeling. I think he sees dead people and talks to them. Mammaw, he knew things he shouldn't have known."

"Nonsense."

"Besides, he said Adam didn't do it." But her grandmother didn't seem to hear.

"Necromancy is what it is. Bringing up the dead when they *should* be left to the Almighty." Mammaw spun the circular cake around to a bare spot. With a sure aim she threw frosting with so much force Cameryn was afraid it would leave a divot. "First Rachel is murdered, then your mother's returned to haunt us and now that boy's arrested. It's like our town's under a curse. I'm glad your father's coming home to help handle it all—he said his business is finally done and no matter what he'll be here tonight. It's all been too much for me."

Cameryn nodded. Pulling back a scarf of hair, she looked out the window. Outside, in whiskey barrels, a few hardy orange and yellow chrysanthemums still clung to life. She knew they would be dead soon, since winter came hard this high in the mountains, and no plant—save the aspen, spruce, and pine—could survive the cold and snow. It made her sad to think of those last few blossoms dying. But then again, she told herself, everything died.

Thursday the town would gather for the funeral, which meant Rachel's body would be sent from Hood Mortuary in Durango to the First Congregational Church of Silverton, where the service would be held.

She didn't want to go to the funeral. Cameryn had been too close to Rachel's body and she couldn't get the images of the autopsy out of her head. Maybe she'd hike alone in the mountains instead, or just stay home and light a candle. But even as she thought it, she knew she *would* be at funeral, because she needed to support Rachel's parents. It was the last thing she could do for her friend.

That, and find her killer.

"I'm not saying I believe in Jewel, Mammaw," Cameryn said carefully, "but like I told you, he knew things. Do you think there's any way Rachel could have spoken through him?"

"Why don't you ask Father Mike?"

Because she didn't want to deal with the endless lectures, she answered silently. And where did her science and its demand for reproducible fact fit in to all this? It was all too confusing. . . .

"What are you thinking of, girl? You're staring out that window like there's an answer there," Mammaw said.

"I don't know. The thing is, I've studied about how psychics do it, and there's lots of ways they trick you. Like the Russian Doll."

"What's that?"

"It's, like, where the psychic says, 'I want to talk about your daughter,' and the person says, 'I don't have a daughter,' so the psychic goes, 'Well, this is someone close to you, that you feel motherly toward, someone *like* a daughter,' and then the person buys into it. I was ready for the tricks, but Jewel didn't do them. I can't understand how he knew so much."

"Smoke and mirrors is what it is."

"What about the Catholic Church? Don't you think in a way we use smoke and mirrors, too? At least incense and gold."

The steel was back in her grandmother. Through tight lips she said, "That's different. The Church doesn't charge the poor and grieving for spiritual help. Dr. Jewel is a shark preying on the lost, and now he's got you and God knows who else believing his lies. Here, eat this." Her grandmother set down a piece of cake in front of Cameryn. The thick frosting swirled in a pattern that looked like petals, and a fork had been tucked to the side with a napkin folded neatly underneath. "It's my old recipe," she told Cameryn. "Every Mahoney woman knows how to bake this cake. Would you like to try your hand at it?"

"Some other time. You might have to adopt."

Her mammaw sighed heavily while Cameryn took a bite and chewed thoughtfully. "There is one thing you could help me with. Tell me about Saint Christopher."

Her grandmother cut herself a slice and sat next to her at the table. "What about him?"

"Justin asked me who Saint Christopher was and I couldn't remember. In all four deaths a Saint Christopher medal was left behind, so I figure that's got to mean something. Justin said Saint Christopher was a demoted saint. Is he?"

"Demoted?" Mammaw shook her head and said, "No, Saint Christopher's still a saint in good standing. In my day his mass used to be celebrated on July twenty-fifth. But there were too many saints and not enough days to celebrate them, so thanks to the Second Vatican Council the poor man got moved off the regular liturgical calendar."

"What's he a saint of again?"

"Travelers."

"That's interesting, since all of the bodies were found in different states. The killer must get around."

Squinting at the window, Mammaw said, "Look, someone's coming up the drive." She pushed her glasses farther up her nose. "Wonder who it is? I don't recognize the car...."

When Cameryn looked out her heart skipped sideways. "It's Justin," she answered.

"Deputy Crowley! Were you expecting him?"

"No."

Mammaw shook her head, her face grim. "Then I don't think you should speak with him, not until you and your father have a chance to discuss that letter." She rose to her feet. "I'll go see what he wants."

"It's okay," Cameryn said quickly. "I want to talk to him."

"You'll talk to him here, in the kitchen."

"No, outside. I'll be fine, Mammaw. I'm sure he's here about the case."

Her grandmother looked skeptical.

"I won't discuss the letter. I want to know what's going on with Adam—that's all. You need to let me do this."

"I'm not thinking of interfering, I'm trying to protect you."

"I don't need protecting, Mammaw."

"Your father won't like that Justin's here and you're not listening to me. It's that streak from your moth—" The word suddenly died in her throat. Her grandmother clapped her lips together and went to the sink, picking up the frosting bowl before setting it down in the exact same place. She turned on the faucet. "All right then," she said, her back still turned. "Do whatever it is you're needing to do."

Cameryn understood this: It was her grandmother's

way of trying not to fight. There had been a subtle shift somewhere, a change in the balance. When had it happened? Whatever its cause, Cameryn felt a surge of gratitude. Hurrying over to the sink, she entwined her arms around her mammaw and quickly kissed her cheek.

"What's that for?" Mammaw asked without turning her head.

"For understanding that I'm growing up. For letting me make my own decisions."

Mammaw lifted a sudsy finger and pressed it gently on the tip of Cameryn's nose. "Growing up, but not grown," she said. "There's a difference. Remember that."

"I'll remember."

Justin had stepped away from his car, and Cameryn could see him from where she stood. He looked as though he fit in Colorado, with his battered red Subaru and faded jeans. She watched him as he made his way toward the house, took in his easy movements that were almost graceful. His feet crunched the gravel as he approached. She was about to open the door when Mammaw blurted, "Your mind is strong but you need to watch your spirit. Guard your heart, girl. Think first."

Confused, Cameryn replied, "If you think I'm attracted to Justin you're wrong."

"I didn't get this old without knowing certain things. Just guard your heart." Her grandmother turned back to the sink.

The knocking came and Cameryn opened the door. Justin was wearing his same uniform of shirt and jeans, but this time he had on an official bomber jacket with a star embroidered on the outside pocket. A pair of aviator sunglasses shrouded his eyes, and in his hand he clutched a large manila envelope. "Hey," he said.

"Hey yourself," Cameryn answered through the screen. "What are you doing here?"

"Your pop faxed the preliminary coroner's report on Rachel and, well, there's something in it I wanted to run by you. Since you're the wannabe forensic guru, I thought you might be able to help."

Cameryn, aware her grandmother was listening to every word, leaned closer. "My dad should be back any minute and he won't like it if you're here."

Justin leaned in, too, on his side of the door. "No worries," he said. "I'll be ready to peel out of the driveway. I'm very fast."

"How's Adam doing?"

"His dad showed up and the questions were flying. I guess you already know about Rachel's shrine, and when you combine it with the witness that saw him, well, it doesn't look so good."

"What's happening now?"

"His dad said his kid needed a lawyer so that's pretty much the end of it. Once a suspect bring lawyers up everything's over. Lyric's there, too." He waggled the report in the air. "So, what do you say? Will you help me?"

She could sense he was reading her closely, watching her for a reaction, gauging how they were going to treat each other since he'd shared the information about Hannah. And the way she was going to handle it was to send all that emotion reflexively underground. She was a professional talking about the case, that was all.

"All right, let's do it," she said. Justin began to open the screen door to enter the kitchen. "Nope, other way," Cameryn corrected him. She grabbed her jacket off a hook and said, "Follow me." They hurried along the pavestones to the edge of the yard where their glider sat beneath a cluster of large aspen. She liked it here, because there was no window facing this part of the yard. The glider was private.

Leaves had landed on the seat, so Justin brushed them off, and they fell like giant snowflakes onto the ground. He took off his sunglasses and she could see the question in his eyes, could see the outer calm that hid what he felt churning beneath his surface. He took a step toward her, and Cameryn took a step back.

"About the other day," he began. "The way we left it, I—"

But Cameryn cut him off. "No. I can't do it, Justin. I haven't talked to my dad yet and I just can't do it. Not now. Tell me about the case."

"Before you shoot me completely down, can we at least

sit?" he asked, pointing to the cleared-off swing.

"Sure." She sat down, and he sat next to her, closer, she realized, than he needed to. Silently Justin handed Cameryn the envelope. She opened it and pulled out the first report, skimming through the cause of death, which was listed as strangulation, to the manner, which was homicide, and then down to the toxicology levels. Most of the blanks had not been filled in, and Cameryn knew those omissions were because the tests would take days to complete. The rape test, however, had come back negative.

"We know none of the other Christopher victims were sexually assaulted, right?" she asked as she flipped to the next page.

"Why can't we just talk?" His voice was soft, pleading. "I won't bite."

She looked up at him and kept her gaze steady. "None of the other Christopher Killer victims were sexually assaulted. Is that right?"

Justin raised one eyebrow, a lone comma on his forehead. "All right, we'll do this your way," he said. She could tell he was disappointed. Shifting gears, the tone of his voice seemed to change. The urgency was gone, replaced by a clinical, almost antiseptic sound. "I checked everything I could find on the other cases, and it's like Jacobs told us at autopsy. None of the girls were assaulted. So, that leaves us with pretty much nothing. I mean, what's the motive here?"

"The killer could be female."

"I thought of that, too. But that's not a profile that fits. Women pretty much aren't serial killers, not unless they're going along with some man."

"What about the Aileen Wuornos case?" Cameryn countered. "They even made a movie about her and the actress who played Wuornos won an Academy Award. Wuornos was a woman and a serial killer."

"You're right. But in the Wuornos case the woman started off killing her tricks. See? Right off you got your motive. In this case I think our perp's a man, but he's a sicko without any kind of reason to kill that anyone can tell." Justin leaned back into the glider and rested his head on its top rung. With his neck stretched that way, she saw a faint mark at the base of his neck, a scratch that almost blended into tan skin, no thicker than a pencil lead. "So what's the story here?" he went on. "And what's up with the medal? It makes no sense."

"I think the killer's trying to leave some sort of message. I found out Saint Christopher is still a saint and he was used as a protection for travelers. It could mean the killer's from far away."

"A traveler. Interesting." Justin stretched out his legs, as if he were talking about the clouds instead of discussing a killer.

"Do you know where the other murders happened?" Cameryn asked.

"Actually, I've got a map here, with the locations marked. There doesn't seem to be a pattern that I can tell. See what you think." He reached inside the manila envelope and handed Cameryn a Xeroxed map. Four different locations had been starred, and next to the stars were names. Hillary Rogers, 19, Plano, Texas. Candace Jones, 17, Braxton, West Virginia. Dawn Kennedy, 22, Albany, New York. And now, the newest star, Rachel Geller, 18, Silverton, Colorado. She had wondered if the other victims had been from small towns, too, but Plano and Albany were big cities, although she wasn't sure about Braxton. And Justin was right—there didn't seem to be a pattern, at least not one that was obvious.

"Okay, new question. Do you know anything about the difference between an organized and a disorganized killer?" he asked her.

"A little." She gave the glider a kick so she could move, since she did her best thinking when she was in motion. In her mind she pictured her *Practical Homicide Investigation* book, the one that graphically showed forensic techniques as well as real homicide scenes. With its explicit black-and-white photos and detailed profiles, her *PHI* was the roughest and most useful of her resource materials. It was the book her mammaw had tried to throw away. Cameryn had fished it out from underneath a pizza box, and it still smelled like onions.

Squinting, she pictured the list. "I know disorganized

killers are loners," she recited. "They usually live close to the crime scene and, let me think . . . they're night people, right? I mean, they like to go out at all hours, to bars and stuff. And, um, I think the book said they internalize their emotions, like hurt and anger. They tend to look different, too." She stopped then, picturing Adam. That first time she'd picked him up he'd talked about visiting Hillside Cemetery and hanging out in the basement of the souvenir shop. No matter what the explanation, he *had* put up photographs of Rachel. Plus he was a loner, which by definition put him on the fringes of normal, which meant in at least a few ways he fit the disorganized profile.

"Anything else?" he asked.

Cameryn hesitated. "Disorganized killers are considered the weird ones in the neighborhood. They're males. They're not educated, they have no close personal friends, and are usually between the ages of seventeen and twenty-five."

Justin smiled at her. "Bravo," he said. "That's very good. No wonder your pop hired you."

But Cameryn waved the compliment away. It wasn't hard to figure out the direction of this conversation. "So what you're saying is that you think Adam's the killer. You think he fits the profile of the disorganized offender. You think he's a copycat who built a shrine to Rachel and when she rejected him he killed her and put a Christopher medal on her to throw the police off the trail."

"I didn't say that. Adam clammed right up when his dad arrived and demanded a lawyer—some high-powered woman from Durango. Don't put words in my mouth, Cameryn. The reason I'm here has to do with these reports. Look." He put the stem of the sunglasses between his teeth as he opened the manila envelope and murmured, "I had these documents faxed this morning and . . . Are you even listening to me?"

She wasn't, at least not completely. Her thoughts worked quickly, one idea morphing into another, and she wanted to follow their lead. "Albany. One of the girls that was killed was from Albany."

"I want to talk to you about the coroner's report."

"All right, all right, I'm listening."

A voice drifted from the back door. "Yoo-hoo, Cameryn, are you getting too cold out there? I made some hot chocolate." Mammaw stood by the kitchen door, her posture ramrod straight. She clutched two mugs, one in each hand.

"No thanks, Mammaw," Cameryn called back. "We're fine."

Even from the distance she could tell her grandmother was giving Justin a hard look. "You're sure, Cammie?"

"Positive. Thanks anyway."

"All right. Come inside if you get too chilled."

"We will. Bye, Mammaw."

Justin pushed the glider and chewed the stem of his

sunglasses. "Well, it doesn't take a great detective to figure out she doesn't like me," he said as the screen door
slammed shut.

"Nope. She doesn't trust you. Neither does my dad. They
both think you're up to no good."

He looked disappointed, but only for a moment.
"Actually, I would have liked that hot chocolate," he said,
and dropped the sunglasses into his pocket. "Let's get
back to the case."

Cameryn said, "By the way, just so you know, Dr. Jewel
doesn't think it's Adam. He said so in his reading after
you left. He said Rachel told him the killer is still in
Silverton and will kill again."

Justin put his foot down and stopped the glider, which
caused Cameryn to rock forward. "Believe it or not, I
think he's right. It's not Adam. I just don't think he's our
guy."

"Why do you say that?"

"A couple of things. First of all, I believe the perp's an
organized offender. Jacobs's looking at Adam first and the
killing scene second. That's backwards. What do you
remember about organized killers?"

"Um, they're smart. They fit in well with society. They're
the type of people you want to be friends with, but they're
really self-centered. They're almost always male, older
than the disorganized killer. And I think they try to
involve themselves with the police investigation."

"Exactly!" Justin turned to face her. "That's a completely different profile than Adam. Think about the crime scene. The killer used duct tape to bind Rachel's hands, which shows the need for control, and control equals organized. And another thing—the perp had to think ahead to bring the duct tape, which shows planning, which again points to organized."

"Rachel's body was laid out carefully, with her hair combed and her feet positioned. Isn't that the kind of stuff an organized killer does? And leaving the Christopher medal's another organized thing to do," she added excitedly, "because they like to 'make a statement.' Leaving the medal is a pretty big statement, don't you think?"

Justin seemed impressed. "And I thought you were just interested in cutting people up."

Cameryn smiled at this. "A forensic pathologist has to learn to read the clues off the body. If you don't, you won't be able to process it right. Like I said, I study."

"Which brings me back to why I'm here," he told her. "Organized, disorganized—that'll only take us so far. I want to go with facts. Look at this partial tox screen." He moved closer, and she could feel his arm against hers, could smell the scent of his soap. As his index finger ran down the front page until it hit a bright yellow line, she noticed that Justin chewed his fingernails. "Begin with Rachel's blood work—there, on line twelve."

Drowned in bright yellow ink were the typed words "Rohypnol (flunitrazepam)." She looked at him blankly. "I'm sorry, Justin. If I'm supposed to know what these are, I don't."

"Rohypnol is a benzodiazepine that is also known by the street names of roofies or R-2. You know, the date-rape drug?"

"What?"

"Rachel was drugged, Cammie. Someone jacked up her drink. You're a waitress at the Grand—do you ever leave your own drink out on the counter while you're working? Because the way I see it, the perp could have slipped a roofie into her drink and waited for her to close the restaurant. This is a fairly low level of drug—it would have made her woozy and maybe a little sick. In that state she probably would have walked right off with the guy."

"Except servers aren't allowed to drink on duty—at least where the customers can see. Sodas are in the back only."

"Hmmm. Well, somehow the perp got it in her drink. And it gets even stranger." Justin's brow furrowed in concentration as he pulled more papers from inside the envelope. "What I'm going to tell you now is something that you can tell no one else."

Cameryn raised her eyebrows. "Okay."

"I'm serious, Cameryn. I could get in big trouble for showing you this. It's information from the other Christopher cases. Law enforcement holds back certain things from the media to protect the integrity of the case if they go to trial. You can't let this out to *anyone*."

"I won't." Cameryn crossed her heart. "I swear."

"These are the coroner reports from the other victims." He pointed to the second page. "Look where I highlighted. It's the same on all of them."

The outdoor sounds—the creaking of the glider, the rustling of the trees—seemed to fade into silence as she read one brightly highlighted area, then another. She flipped through the other coroner reports. *Flunitrazepam, flunitrazepam, flunitrazepam*—each murdered girl had been given date-rape drugs.

"One of the other victims was a waitress like Rachel, another worked at a Seven-Eleven, and the third was a maid in a hotel. Four girls on low levels of date-rape drugs, guaranteed to make them compliant."

Justin tapped the reports. "For once you're not connecting the dots. The information on the roofies wasn't released to the media. A copycat killer could place a Christopher medal on a victim, easy, but how would he know to use the drug? Rachel was another victim from the *same* serial killer."

"So it's not Adam," Cameryn breathed.

"No. Jewel was right."

Sounds came rushing back as Cameryn's mind began to whirr again. It wasn't Adam. The drug suggested a person with at least some city experience, and leaving the medal behind suggested a traveler. . . . She chewed the edge of her lip. "I know I've asked you this before, but Dr. Jewel knows a lot about the murder. Could it be him?"

"Again, I thought of that, but we checked him out just like all the other police did in all the other cases. Unless he can kill someone from a distance using nothing but psychic powers, he's not our man. I checked all the airlines and he didn't fly out of New Mexico, period. Ditto with buses, which don't even run to Silverton. I checked every single car rental in New Mexico and the man didn't rent a pogo stick. Just in case, I ran all the car rental *returns* during the time frame and got nada. Not to mention the witness who said he was there at the conference. Jewel's clean."

"Well, how can you explain the things he said about Rachel? He said he knew she dyed her hair. He said she had on hoop earrings with green beads. How could he have known all that?"

Justin paused. "He couldn't have. I think he's the real deal."

But Cameryn was taking in something new, Justin's dirt-covered license plate. Something registered in her mind. Something Dr. Jewel had said . . .

Her face must have changed, because Justin asked, "What's wrong, Cammie? You look like you just saw a ghost."

"I'm sorry, I'm just . . . tired. It's been a hard day. I think maybe I should go in now." She looked again at the mark on his neck, the bit of pink that stretched up his neck like a snake's tail. And it felt like that very snake was coiling inside her, knotting her together.

His gaze followed hers. "You're looking at the scratches? I was pruning trees for my landlady. I guess I'm not very good at it." He flipped up the collar of his jacket.

"Yeah," she said. "Well, my dad's going to be here any second, so—"

"So you're telling me I should go before I cause problems. No worries. I certainly don't want to overstay my welcome." He stood, and the glider did a crazy dance before Cameryn steadied it. The sun was behind Justin, wiping out his features as his frame cast a shadow over her. She looked up at him.

"You're sure you're all right?" he asked again.

She made herself smile. "Positive. Can I keep this map? The one that shows where the victims died?"

"Sure. I've got copies at the station. Okay, then. Well, I'll just get on back to Sheriff Jacobs. Make sure you stay out of trouble."

"I will," she nodded. At that moment nothing made sense. She was a scientist, a skeptic, and yet there seemed to be proof that Jewel was real. Justin believed in him. So did Lyric. And in some ways Jewel seemed to meet the burden of proof that science demanded. Still, the idea of a psychic getting signs from the dead went against everything she believed in. Her mind reeled as she tried to separate the fact from the fantasy.

"You promise to stay out of trouble?" Justin pressed.

"I promise."

"Good."

She watched as he walked to the edge of her driveway. He gave her a tiny wave, touching his fingers to his forehead, then slid into the seat of his Subaru. She looked at the map, at the star on Albany, the place where Justin had been raised, and West Virginia, just a heartbeat away from the Blue Ridge Mountains where Justin admitted he'd traveled on his motorcycle. He'd been in the area where two of the murders had occurred. But that in itself meant nothing. Millions of people had connections like that. It was the piece that Jewel had divined that tied it all together.

Justin tapped his horn twice as he pulled away. His tires spun a small cloud of dirt that hung in the air, almost covering the New York license plate.

The plate, on Justin's car, had an *M* in its center. It was blue. Exactly as Dr. Jewel had said.

Chapter Thirteen

JEWEL'S ASSISTANT STEPHANIE WAITED in the lobby of the Grand, talking to the owner's daughter in an animated conversation that Cameryn guessed had to do with ghosts. Stephanie had changed into a camel-colored pantsuit, a designer outfit that pinched her waist and flared over her small hips. Gone were the chopstick hairpins. In their place was a single gold bar, like a Mayan ingot, and diamonds that sparkled from her lobes. When she saw Cameryn, Stephanie quickly excused herself and hurried to where Cameryn stood. Cameryn had called from the road.

"You're sure this is an emergency?" was Stephanie's greeting.

"Yes. Like I said, I'm working the case." Cameryn tried to sound calm, but she was afraid Stephanie would be able to read the hammering of her heart. Lifting her chin, she said, "It's important I talk to Dr. Jewel."

"Personally, I would have said no, but Dr. Jewel is soft-hearted. We can't take too long, though. Tight schedule and all. Follow me."

As Stephanie began to walk through the lobby toward the stairs, her tone became more conversational. "I was just hearing stories about the Grand—did you know there are three spirits that haunt this place?"

Cameryn glanced at the ceiling above. "Three ghosts?"

"Yes, three. That girl behind the counter?"

"Diane—"

"Diane told me she hears them at night, creaking doors and slamming drawers. I explained to her she's got to call out to the spirits, really loud, and tell them, 'You're dead. You need to pass on to the light.' Sometimes the spirits get confused and don't know where they are. You've got to let them know it's okay to move on to the next dimension. That happened to your friend Rachel."

"It did?"

"When she came to Dr. Jewel he explained to her that she'd passed on. Rachel had been caught halfway between this world and the next. Poor child didn't know where she was. Shall we?" she said, sweeping her arm up the staircase. Nervous, Cameryn followed.

The worn, flowered carpeting was so padded it muffled every step, and Cameryn had always thought the gilded handrail, curved and golden, would have been more suited to an opera house. The Grand was a time capsule of a building—nothing had been changed much since Wyatt Earp left his bullet hole over the bar. The second floor had an old-fashioned lobby filled with backless couches. Each had been upholstered in wine-colored velvet dimpled with buttons, set in polite lines against three of the four walls. The lounges were relics from a bygone era, a time when ladies received visitors in a neutral space because they would never allow an unrelated male to enter their rooms.

She took in the striped wallpaper laced with faded, yellowed roses, and the windows from the late 1800s, made of glass as thin as rice paper. Although she worked in the restaurant, Cameryn had rarely been in the hotel side of the building.

"Diane said one of the ghosts that haunts this place is a doctor," Stephanie went on. "The lady who hanged herself in room thirty-three is still here, too. They found her in the closet with a belt around her neck and the word 'good-bye' written in lipstick on the vanity mirror. Jewel's been trying to contact her but he thinks she's already passed into the light."

Cameryn fought the urge to turn and run. Was she really buying into this craziness? And yet there were so many facts that couldn't be explained. No, she had to see it through, no matter where it led. They stopped at room 23.

Rapping her knuckle gently on the door, Stephanie announced, "We're here, Dr. Jewel. It's Stephanie. I've brought Cameryn Mahoney."

A moment later the door swung open and Dr. Jewel ushered them inside, saying, "Yes, please come in. I'm afraid I'm in a terrible rush so I don't have much time. We'll have to talk in here." He wore the same tunic he had worn earlier, but now he wore ankle boots with zippers on the side. He flashed a smile, but his eyes seemed guarded.

"Cameryn's here to talk about the Christopher Killer," Stephanie said. "Her father's the coroner, remember? She said she had some questions."

"Ah, yes," he said, nodding, "of course. Have a seat, Cameryn. I'm afraid the accommodations are not the best, but these old hotels have a lot more spiritual energy than a plain old Hyatt. Please," he said, pointing to a small sofa, "sit."

Cameryn dropped into the love seat while Stephanie perched on the end of the bed. Jewel sat on an uncomfortable-looking chair that creaked beneath his weight. The man looked different up close. The skin on Jewel's face was much more sallow than it had appeared at a distance, and there were bags beneath his eyes that had been undetectable under the show's blazing lights. His sleek hair, scrupulously brushed for the camera, now appeared rougher, less sculpted, tumbling forward toward his chin. But his smile was still broad and the teeth had their same, unnatural whiteness.

"So, refresh my mind. Your father's the coroner, and the two of you worked on Rachel's remains, correct?"

"Yes. I work with my father as his assistant. I'm assistant to the coroner."

Dr. Jewel looked impressed. "That's extraordinary for a girl your age. Before we get to your questions I'd like to ask you about the crime scene. I'm curious, you see, to compare my impressions with the actual facts. Sort of a psychic check-up, if you will, to see how accurate my reading was."

"You already know it was accurate. You 'saw' Rachel's body and the Christopher medal. We found her just like you said."

"My accuracy troubles you. And there's so much more, isn't there?"

Cameryn could sense Jewel's excitement as he asked this—from the way he leaned toward her, his elbows drilling his knees, his chin resting on the bridge of his fingers, it seemed as though he could hardly contain himself. In a flash she realized his desire to pump her for information was probably the reason he'd agreed to see her. But she knew how dangerous it was to give out details, especially when the killer was still free. Shaking her head, she answered, "I'm sorry, Dr. Jewel, but it's like I said when you were taping the show—I can't talk to you about the details of the case."

Dr. Jewel bent forward cozily. "I won't tell anyone," he told her softly.

"I'm . . . I'm sorry."

The smile deflated. They stared at each other in silence until finally he broke it by saying, "Well, maybe as you learn to trust me you'll change your mind. You are a very guarded person, Cameryn. I understand you've always been a bit of a skeptic."

Cocking her head, Cameryn asked, "And you know this how?"

"Because Rachel's telling me right now."

Cameryn blinked. Goose bumps pricked her flesh. "She's here?"

"Yes. As well as another female presence." Dr. Jewel straightened himself and leaned into the back of the chair. "The second one's a little girl. She's standing to the side of you, your left side, actually, and she's got her hand on your shoulder. Does this make sense to you?"

Instinctively, Cameryn whipped her head to the left, but saw nothing more than an old-fashioned lamp shade with a beaded fringe.

"She's a little dark-haired girl, probably no more than three years of age. She's wearing some sort of pink jump-suit. Do you understand this?" He slid easily into his *Shadow of Death* banter. "I'm listening," he said.

"I don't know about any little girl."

"Doesn't matter—she seems to know you."

Cameryn shrugged, feeling silly about the conversation. "I don't know what to say. Maybe she's a friend of Rachel's. Maybe they met on the other side."

Dr. Jewel smiled tolerantly. "That's not it. But, seeing as I don't have much time, why don't you tell me why you are here. I'm listening."

Why *was* she here? Sitting on the sofa, under the gaze of Stephanie and Dr. Jewel, Cameryn began to wonder at the stupidity of her plan. Even as she prepared to articulate her questions, she desperately wanted everything she was thinking to be wrong. The emotions fighting inside her were like waves, each one swelling up and replacing the tide that had come before: fear, condemnation, skepticism, doubt, attraction. The last emotion was the hardest for her to deal with, because Mammaw had been right: Cameryn hadn't guarded her heart.

She pictured Justin with his blue-green eyes, the patient way he talked to her and his slow smile. It was impossible to plumb what being right would mean.

Out on the glider, when she'd talked with Justin, her thoughts seemed clear enough. One thing she hadn't listed under characteristics of an organized killer was their choice of profession. Hadn't the book said that organized offenders chose jobs that projected a "macho" image, like a police officer? The exact job Justin had.

The scratches teased her. They could have been caused by trimming branches, exactly as he claimed, but what if they were from Rachel? She pictured Rachel struggling, her fingernails clawing as she gasped for air, and the image made her shudder. At the autopsy they'd clipped Rachel's nails and sent the little slivers to the lab. But the DNA results wouldn't be back for weeks. In the meantime, what if Justin disappeared? Or worse, killed again?

And there was more: Justin lived in the East, where two of the murders had happened. Hadn't he lived in Albany? And his trip to the Blue Ridge Mountains placed him close to Braxton, West Virginia. Worse still, a girl in Silverton died the week after he came to town. But it was the letter *M* that made all the pieces click together. Jewel had thrown that letter out at the reading, the very letter on Justin's New York license plate.

The bigger part of her believed crime was solved by science, not mystics, and the science side of her laughed at her own naïveté. But hadn't Jewel proven himself by knowing about Rachel's dyed hair? And what about the hoop earrings? A real scientist followed the evidence, no matter what. If Dr. Jewel was genuine, she needed to follow the thread that led to Justin. No matter what the cost.

"Talk to me," Jewel prompted.

"Um, you say Rachel's here in this room?" Cameryn began. Her voice had a slight tremor, betraying her nervousness. She could feel her palms dampen with sweat, so she rubbed them against her knees as she watched Dr. Jewel watch her.

Sitting on the bed, Stephanie had crossed her legs; her

foot, sheathed in a high-heel shoe, jiggled back and forth as though it had a life of its own. "I'm sorry," she said, "but I've just got to ask the obvious. Why are you here, Cameryn? You don't believe. Jewel has proven himself again and again, but still you doubt." Her voice was impatient. "If he sees a little girl, you can count on a little girl here with some connection to you. If he says Rachel's here, you can count on it. What's it going to take for you to trust him?"

"I'm *trying*, okay?" Cameryn said. "This is all very new to me."

Dr. Jewel stared at her, impassive. "Of course I understand your skepticism. It's natural for a person raised in a rigid faith system. But believe this: I'm looking right at Rachel, at this very moment. She's extending a teddy bear to you, which is her way of saying she gives you warmth and comfort from beyond."

Cameryn pushed her hand toward Jewel as though she held up a stop sign. "Okay, ask her to tell me the name of her killer."

Dr. Jewel rose from the chair. He went to the small wooden nightstand and picked up a glass already filled with water. A jar sat next to the water, and next to that sat a spoon, which he dipped into the jar labeled DMSO. After dumping the contents into the glass, he stirred the water vigorously. The cloud of white disappeared almost immediately. "For my stomach," he apologized.

"Dr. Jewel is under too much stress," Stephanie explained. "Speaking to the dead is hard work. No one appreciates the toll it takes on the man."

"Now, to your question. I can't give you a name. To put it simply, psychic energy isn't as easy to read as, say, regular language we might speak."

"People don't understand about Dr. Jewel," Stephanie said. "They think he just listens to the spirits while they talk in words. It's not like that. The dead are trying to send impressions, and it can be like trying to read a newspaper underwater. Things get distorted. That's why Dr. Jewel needs his cleansing period—"

"Cleansing period?" Cameryn asked.

"You don't know much about his work, do you? Dr. Jewel goes away, by himself, with no human contact or food for twenty-four hours—not even water. During that time of deprivation he centers himself so he can hear the vibrations from the spirits. He had a cleansing period in Santa Fe before Rachel came to him. That's why he could hear her so clearly."

"Exactly," agreed Jewel. He looked at Cameryn expectantly. Then, draining the glass, he wiped his lips with the back of his hand. "But even now I can read you, Cameryn. You're wondering if the killer is someone from Silverton, aren't you?" He set the glass down and then turned to her. "You're afraid it's someone you know, perhaps, someone you like. That thought is hard for you."

Cameryn felt her heart jump as she formed the next question. "I want to ask you about the letter *M*. You mentioned that letter this morning and I . . . Can you . . . can you ask Rachel about that? Please, it's very important."

"She's right here," Jewel replied. "Ask her yourself."

Cameryn shook her head. "Would you do it? Please?"

Sighing, Dr. Jewel said, "Very well. As I explained, Rachel has already heard the question. Spirits aren't deaf, you know." He squeezed his eyes shut, frowning for a moment in concentration. When he opened his eyes again, they had grown soft with appeal as he whispered, "I'm sorry, Rachel, I don't understand."

"What's she saying?" Cameryn asked. Her nerves pulsated with energy.

"I can't get her to acknowledge the letter *M*. She's saying the little girl with her wants to come through. The little girl wants to speak to you, Cameryn."

"I told you, I don't know about any little girl! That's not what I'm here for."

"And I told you I can't control what the spirits say. Rachel's insisting on bringing the girl through."

Cameryn's eyes drifted once again to the nightstand, and as they did, something fell into place. A piece of information, one she'd forgotten she knew, now surfaced from her memory, like a fin breaking the surface of the water. And then there was a soft rapping on the door, and a female voice announced that the news crew was waiting downstairs in the main lobby. Instantly on her feet, Stephanie smoothed her hair and tugged her jacket while checking herself in the small vanity mirror.

"Well, that means our time's up," said Jewel. "I'm sorry it was so short. I hope I've been helpful."

"You have," Stephanie told him, before Cameryn could reply.

Dr. Jewel stopped in front of Cameryn, towering over her like a totem, his expression carved in wood. He took her arm and helped her to her feet. His hand felt dry and strong against her skin. Rubbing his thumb over the back of her hand, he said, "I understand how difficult it is to lose someone you care about, but remember, you needn't fear death. There's life beyond. Hold on to that. And don't be afraid to believe. You can have faith and science, too."

"I'll remember," Cameryn told him. "I think I understand a lot, now. Much more than before I came in." Pulling her hand free, she said, "Good luck on your interview."

The three of them stepped into the hallway; Dr. Jewel locked the door with his old-fashioned key that dangled from a large key ring. "I hope Rachel comes through when I'm on camera," he said. "That's what the newspeople want to see. The spirits can be so temperamental."

"Are you going to walk down with us?" Stephanie asked. She had taken a comb from her purse and was fixing the doctor's hair. He had to bend at the knees for her to reach the top of his head.

Cameryn answered, "No. I need to make a quick call. You two go on."

"Good-bye, then," Dr. Jewel told her as he straightened. "I wish you the best in finding your murderer."

Cameryn watched as Stephanie, precarious on her pencil-thin heels, and Dr. Jewel, moving with elegant posture, descended the winding stairs to the reporters below. When they were out of sight she checked to see if anyone else was around. The lobby was empty, with only the rubber plant nodding in the corner as a witness. Pulling her cell phone from her back pocket, she quickly punched in the sheriff's number, her heart thumping so hard she could feel the beat in her ears.

After three rings she heard, "Hello?"

The voice on the other end didn't belong to Sheriff Jacobs. Biting her lip, she said, "Hello, Justin? It's me, Cameryn. I need Dr. Moore's number. Fast."

With a pen she wrote the number on her hand as Justin obediently recited it back to her. "What's going on, Cameryn?" he asked. "What are you up to? You're hyperventilating."

"Nothing," she lied. She slipped the pen back into her pocket and made one more sweep of the Grand. It was empty save for the fan spinning gently from the ceiling.

"Come on, give it up," Justin said. "You were weird on

the swing and now you're acting even stranger. Something's up," he told her. "I can feel it."

"I said it's nothing."

"And I'm saying you're a bad liar. I just helped you with Moore's number, so it's only fair you keep me in the loop. What's going on?"

"I'm not sure yet." She hesitated. Her hands shook and she knew she was clutching the phone too hard. "I need to check something first. That's why I've got to talk to Moore."

"What thing?"

"Justin—I think . . ." She hesitated. It seemed strange to utter the phrase out loud, but this time, forensically, the pieces fit. She was no longer dependant on Jewel's fantastic claims. Now she was back in the world of science. "If I'm right," she blurted out, "swear to God, I may have just found Rachel's killer."

Chapter Fourteen

"CAMERYN MAHONEY!" DR. MOORE BARKED into her phone. "What in the name of Pete do you want?"

Since they hadn't left on the best of terms, Cameryn didn't want to raise his hackles any further. Trying to keep her voice bright, she repeated, "Like I said, I just need to ask you one quick question. I really am sorry to bother you, Dr. Moore, but—"

Without waiting for her to finish, Dr. Moore broke in, "You do realize, don't you, that you're interrupting my work? I've got a suicide with a bullet hole in his head and two naturals to autopsy, not to mention a mound of paper to slog through that reaches clear to the ceiling. I'll talk to you as long as you don't waste my time."

"My question has to do with the Geller case—"

"Too late. The body's already shipped off to the funeral home. Anything else?"

Cameryn spun around, her cell phone planted tight in her ear, afraid to be overheard. Downstairs the interview with Denver's NBC channel and *Shadow of Death* was in full swing—although she could hear no sound at all from below. The Grand, always sparsely occupied during the weekends, was completely devoid of weekday customers, which made the hotel feel even more like a mausoleum. From Lyric, who got her information directly from Daphne, Cameryn knew that except for Dr. Jewel the second floor was completely empty of guests. The doors to the other rooms were closed, mute and silent, lidded eyes shut in slumber. Still, she felt cautious at the thought of being overhead. Dropping her voice low, she said, "What I want to know has to do with DMSO. Do you know anything about it?"

"Dimethyl sulfoxide? It's a solvent, a by-product of the paper pulp industry that started way back in the Eighteen Hundreds." She thought she could hear papers shuffling. "If you've got a question about its properties then go to the library," he told her, distracted. "I'm not your personal encyclopedia. Good-bye, Ms. Mahoney."

"No, *wait!*"

There was a beat. "Yes?"

"I was with Dr. Jewel and he mixed some DMSO in his drink. He said it was for his stomach. I know they use it for horses and things—"

"—and for digestion, for scleroderma, urogenital disorders, and even as an anti-inflammatory drug. As far as

Jewel taking it, what can I say? People do all kinds of strange things in the name of health. Now you can answer *my* question: Why were you even talking with the so-called doctor? That's not the job of a forensic pathologist."

Cameryn shifted from foot to foot. "Um . . . I had a lead. At least, at first, I thought it was a lead. But then I talked to Jewel and it didn't pan out," she confessed. "Then when I saw the DMSO on his nightstand, well, it got me thinking along a whole other line. That's why I called you."

"Back up." Cameryn could imagine Dr. Moore's look as he barked, "You were in the bedroom of a charlatan who is, most likely, as crazy as a loon. Do you think that was wise, Ms. Mahoney? To me that seems an appalling lack of judgment."

"I didn't go in his room alone," she answered, her voice rising. "His assistant Stephanie was there with us the whole time. Besides, what difference does it make if I go into someone's room?"

"You just made my point for me. Let me be direct here: You're a high-school kid who's overestimated herself. You can't even stay on task—you've gone from forensic pathologist to detective in the span of three short days! Goodbye, Ms. Mahoney."

She could feel him getting ready to hang up. "No," she quickly pleaded. "All right, all right, I'm sorry. I *apologize* for my tone. I'm just kind of tense right now." Shaking her head, she said, "Look, what I need is to ask you about DMSO. Can you help me? Please?"

He seemed to wait a moment, probably, she thought, to make sure she suffered. Finally a long stream of breath escaped into the mouthpiece of his phone. She could hear his chair squeak. "Let's get on to the precise nature of your DMSO question. And I expect you to be quick about it. One of my naturals is crawling with bugs so I've got to freeze him, which means, as I've already stated, I don't have time for a cozy chat. Go."

Feeling the clock ticking, Cameryn spoke in a rush. "All right, the DMSO chemical pulls things through the skin barrier, right? I mean, I remember when Lyric used it on her horse, but her mom made her wash her hands really carefully before she touched the stuff because she said the DMSO would drag dirt or ink or whatever was on her hands right into her skin. She said it could, like, tattoo Lyric's palms or something. Is that true?"

"Correct. Dimethyl sulfoxide draws elements into the bloodstream right through the skin barrier. But I feel forced at this point to add a big 'so what?' That's one of the properties of DMSO, but certainly not the *only* one. Obviously Dr. Jewel feels it helps his stomach. Maybe one of his ghost friends recommended it for *phantom* pains." He laughed softly at his own joke. "Are we done?"

In the background Cameryn could hear the heavy notes of opera, swelling in funeral waves, which meant Dr. Moore must be preparing to cut. "Okay, here's my question. Does DMSO leave a smell on a person's breath—like a garlic smell?"

The doctor seemed to hesitate. "I'm not an expert on the properties of DMSO, but if memory serves, I believe it leaves a slight odor of garlic that secretes from the digestive track. I suppose you could say that anyone silly enough to drink the stuff gets a side benefit of bad breath. Did your Dr. Jewel need a mint?"

"I knew it, I knew it!" she said excitedly. "Think a minute, Dr. Moore. Think about Rachel." Cameryn felt a surge of energy as her ideas clicked into place in a clear, forensic formula. "Remember what I smelled at the autopsy? I smelled *garlic*!"

"Dear Lord, we're not back to this again! Are you still obsessing about the fact Rachel had a whiff of garlic coming from her lungs? It means nothing!"

"Just hear me out! The tox screen on Rachel showed roofies in her system, right? Well, I'm going to tell you something you can't repeat to anyone else. Okay?" Give him some special information, she calculated. Pull him on to her team. Let the doctor know she trusted him.

"It'll go right into the vault."

Cameryn took a breath. Her legs shook as she said, "What people don't know is that *all* the victims had roofies in their systems, in the same low dose that Rachel had. *What if* that's because the killer mixed his date-rape cocktail into something like a Coke? And then *what if* he added DMSO to the mix?" She could hear the eagerness in her own voice as her words came faster and faster. "And *what if* the killer is, say, in the restaurant, and he waits for *all* the other customers to be leave? *What if*, right then, the killer spilled his own drink, which of course meant the server has to go and clean it up. Wouldn't cleaning up a drink spiked with DMSO pull some of the date-rape drugs into the victim's bloodstream? And wouldn't that make it really easy to get the server under his control? One victim worked at a Seven-Eleven—she'd have to clean up spills. One was a maid, so same for her. Another one of the victims was a *server*, just like Rachel. It really is a perfect plan!"

"You mixed your tenses."

It took a moment for Cameryn to process this. "What?"

"In your scenario. You went from past to present tense. That's poor grammar. Don't they teach you anything in school anymore?"

Stunned, Cameryn asked, "Were you not listening to me?"

"Oh, I was. I think you should give up forensics and detective work and go straight into fiction writing. I've got a bit of skill in that area myself," Dr. Moore told her.

"Try mine out. *What if* aliens from another planet beamed Rachel's body into their spaceship? *What if*, when they were done with their sordid extraterrestrial examination, the aliens decided to kill Rachel so she wouldn't spill the beans about their planet?" His sarcasm was unmistakable now. "And *what if* the aliens put a Saint Christopher medal on her body, who, by the way, I deduce must be the patron saint of the space folk. Hmmm, I think my theory's even better than yours. What do you think, Ms. Mahoney? Is there a Pulitzer in my future? Oh, wait, I'm asking the wrong person. Better ask Dr. Jewel. *He's* the guy who reads tarot cards."

Heat rocketed into Cameryn's cheeks and anger shot behind her eyes like sparklers. He was mocking her. He had blown off every word she'd said. But she still needed him, and that made her madder still. Trying to keep the anger from her voice, she said, "I'm being serious, Dr. Moore. If the killer did it the way I'm saying then it would account for two forensic things: the garlic smell and the color on the palms of Rachel's hands. I'm thinking the color would be from the Coke or root beer passing into the skin. Maybe it sounds a little crazy, but I think it's a theory that might have merit. Could you run a screen for DMSO on her blood?"

"Based on what? On your fairy tale? No, I think I owe our taxpayers more than that."

"How hard would it be—?"

"Not hard, just expensive and unnecessary. Actually, I suspect you've resorted to this kind of invention because, frankly, you didn't contribute at the autopsy. Let me end by saying the operative word in your little scenario is 'might.' You have no proof, none whatsoever, that Dr. Jewel had anything to do with Rachel's death. A bottle of DMSO proves nothing. Your father told me himself that Dr. Jewel was in Santa Fe at the time of the murder. Your wild accusations reveal you to be the immature, inexperienced amateur I thought you to be. Let the police do their work, Ms. Mahoney, and for Pete's sake, let me do mine. Good-bye."

He meant it this time. The dial tone droned in her ear, a single, monotonous note. She would have screamed in frustration, could have because the thick carpeting would have soaked it up, but instead she shoved her phone into her back pocket so hard she heard a thread pop. So, he thought she was an amateur. Dr. Moore had no idea who he was dealing with!

For a moment she paced, utterly frustrated over Moore's blow-off and yet fearful a kernel of truth might be hidden inside his accusations. Everything she'd said had been speculation. But what she'd constructed in her mind made sense of the evidence. The problem was she needed more. If she could find the roofies, she'd have him. He might even have another Christopher medal inside.

There might be duct tape she could trace back to the piece cut from Rachel's hands. And there was only one way to find out.

It wasn't that hard to get the skeleton key—Cameryn worked in the Grand, after all. After chatting up Diane, she offered to cover the desk for a moment so Diane could watch the interview, but only for a minute because Cameryn had to get home. Alone, she pocketed the skeleton key, smooth and cold, as much of a relic as the antique mirror behind the lumbering desk. True to her word, Diane returned in less than five minutes.

"Are they going to interview much longer?" Cameryn asked.

"Oh yeah, looks like they're just getting warmed up. I was hoping to get an autograph but they're too busy. Thanks for letting me take a break, though," Diane said, grateful. The phone rang then. Diane picked it up, giving Cameryn her opportunity.

Unseen, she slipped up the steps, as quiet as the spirits haunting the Grand. With one last sweep of her eyes, she once again cased the second-floor lobby. A gauzy curtain moved in an unseen breeze while dust particles shimmered in a light beam as round as a pillar. It wasn't hard to believe ghosts floated in the Grand's prismatic air. "If you're here, Rachel," she whispered, "help me nail this guy. Just help me."

With a flick of the key the lock sprang; quickly, quietly, she made her way into the room.

It was different now that the room was empty. The place looked older, more tattered, like a well-worn book read countless times before being passed to friends, the kind of book that looked friendly, but used. She took in the mulberry pattern on the bedspread, but she saw not the intricate tapestry design but how the fabric had pilled, as rough as a cat's tongue. Perched on a tall brass frame, the mattress sagged in the middle; the bed skirt frayed at the hem like an old ball gown. The center of the velvet seat had been worn smooth; this was a room clinging to the past. A brass alarm clock, squat on three legs, ticked softly, reminding her she didn't have much time.

The DMSO was still on the nightstand, so she picked it up and examined the label, hoping for clues. *Dimethyl sulfoxide*, she read silently. Holding the amber bottle to the light, she saw it was only half full. Opening the top she sniffed it, but the powder smelled more like over-ripe fruit than garlic. She set it down and began her search.

Drawers first. The old wood resisted as she tugged on it, and when she finally got it opened she realized the workmanship was rough, as though made by a blacksmith instead of a carpenter. Unlined, the first drawer was neatly stacked with Jewel's underthings. One at a time she carefully lifted his boxer shorts, his too-white T-shirts, his meticulously folded socks. Nothing unusual was there.

The next drawer held four pairs of denim jeans, clean and neatly folded. Methodically, she searched the pockets but found nothing. Another drawer had a leather box, the size of a loaf pan. "Come on, come on," she muttered, picturing a Christopher medal. *Let it be in here!* But when she opened it she was disappointed; inside, lying on a bed of heavy black satin, were only four items: two turquoise rings, a thin watch, and a money clip topped with a diamond triangle. Next to the jewelry was a pack of cigarettes, menthol, and a silver lighter etched with the triangle.

"I didn't know you smoked," she murmured. "I suppose if you talk to the dead you're not so worried about dying from cancer."

A cell phone, small and thin, had been perfectly aligned with the jewelry box. Flipping it open, she checked his directory, hoping to find . . . what, exactly? Rachel's number? As she scanned the list she found nothing but a bunch of names she didn't know, plus restaurants and rental-car numbers. Snapping it shut, she placed it by the jewelry box. She was getting nowhere.

There were two glasses cases in the next drawer, one made of molded plastic covered with denim and the other fashioned from real alligator skin. The denim case yielded a pair of glasses with thick plastic frames, a cheap kind of plastic that looked more suitable for a laborer than a psychic. More puzzling still was a second pair of glasses; this pair was sleek, with expensive-looking designer frames and much thinner lenses, nestled neatly in the alligator case. She held one pair to the next and studied them in light from the window. Trying them on, she was able to guess they were the same prescription, but when she looked in the mirror the thick pair distorted her eyes to half their size. Careful, she placed the glasses back, each in their proper case, and snapped the lids shut. Then, in the last drawer, she found a tape recorder. Turning down the volume, she hit PLAY and listened. But instead of a confession or something useful, she heard Jewel's voice, chanting. It sounded like some sort of mantra. She hit FAST-FORWARD and listened again, but it was the same, endless chanting. Rewinding it, she put it back in the drawer and shut it.

The alarm clock told her she'd been inside four minutes. Before she'd opened the door, she'd promised herself to stay inside no more than ten minutes, for safety's sake. *Hurry!* she commanded herself. Although she told herself she was fine because the interview was bound to take much longer, she also wanted to give herself enough time to make it out of the building before Jewel returned. *Tick tick tick tick,* accused the clock. Minutes were passing, and she'd found nothing.

She caught sight of her face, drawn and pale, in the vanity mirror. Looking down, she refused to return that gaze, because she could tell by her wide eyes just how frightened she really was. Sweat gathered at the edges of her hair as the reality screamed inside her head: *You're breaking and entering! You could get arrested! This is illegal!*

He's leaving in an hour; he may have killed Rachel; he could get away with it forever! she hissed back. *Nothing will go wrong if I don't get caught. So don't get caught.*

Her heart began to flutter as fast as the ticks of the alarm clock as she forced herself to move on. The closet was next. Inside it, Jewel had hung a nylon jacket, dark blue with a tan stripe, as well as more of the tunics he seemed to favor, a Nehru-style coat, plus a leather jacket with fringe. Out of place were a long-sleeved blue poplin work shirt and a pair of matching twill pants. Not the kind of style she would have guessed for Jewel, but when she checked the pockets she found nothing. *Tick tick tick tick.* The spit began to dry in her mouth as she patted down the pockets. Her heart leapt when she found a small piece of paper, folded into a square—it turned out to be a receipt from a restaurant in Santa Fe.

She looked to the floor. Pushed to one corner was a suitcase, which she opened and carefully examined. Unzipping every pocket, she ran her hands into emptiness. Above her she could feel the jacket graze her arm as she rezipped the suitcase and returned it to its exact position. To the side of it sat three gray flannel shoe bags.

Inside the first one was a pair of heavy work boots, dusty on the sides with scuffed metal tips. The other bags contained what she expected Jewel to wear: One held an expensive pair of running shoes and the other held another pair of moccasins, this one without beads. Rolling onto her toes, she craned her neck. On the top shelf she spied a baseball cap with some sort of insignia, the kind a workman would wear. *Interesting,* she thought, fingering the brim.

"But I need proof," she said softly. "I need something real so I can prove he did this. Where are the drugs?" But this time she knew she was talking only to herself because Rachel wasn't really here. Jewel had played them all, played Cameryn even when she'd known better. He'd thrown out the Fuzzy Facts and let her read herself. Even the letter *M* came from the Win-Win game. *She herself* had made the connection. The *M* could have stood for "Mammaw," or "mother," or any of a hundred other associations. As for the murders and his amazing accuracy at the crime scene, he had been there, which allowed him to reveal his intimate facts. He'd been looking right at Rachel's hoop earrings when he'd squeezed the life out of her. And there had to be some way to prove it.

The room was absolutely still. She felt the slightest breeze, a kiss of air, coming from the bathroom. The door squeaked as she entered the small, black-and-white-tiled room, as scrupulously neat and inscrutable as Jewel's closet and drawers. Faster now, she searched his toiletry kit, brimming with expensive skin-care lotions and cologne. She was less careful than she had been with his clothes. Rifling through its contents, she was taken aback by the discovery of Chanel mascara, in charcoal, as well as a heavy foundation formulated for maximum coverage of aging skin. Again, there was nothing. She made another sweep, of the bathtub, the nightstands, the closet—everything was clear and straightforward, devoid of any thread of a clue that might wind back to Rachel. So she couldn't prove a thing. She hadn't found a stash of Christopher medals. She hadn't found receipts linking him to Silverton. She hadn't found squat. Frustration welled inside her, jamming her throat. There was nothing here that spoke of a crime. Of course not. He'd been too careful to reveal how he'd been in two places at once. He was too slick to leave a date-rape drug in view. Jewel was an old hand at this game, and he knew how to win.

Suddenly a thought flashed through her, one more place Jewel might have hidden damning evidence: beneath the bed.

She zeroed in on the clock. Her time was up. Eleven minutes had passed since she'd entered Jewel's room, and she knew it would be safest if she left right then, but . . . A second later she dropped to her knees, pulling up the bed skirt to peer beneath.

At first it seemed empty in the half-light. Blinking, she waited for her eyes to adjust. *Tick tick tick tick*, sang the clock from the nightstand. Dust had gathered by one brass leg, like a tiny dune, and the air smelled of ancient sheets and dirty carpet. But there was something she couldn't make out beneath the head of the bed, something the size of a fist. Straining, pushing herself underneath, her hand reached to grasp the object, but her fingertips moved it just beyond reach. By kicking her legs she propelled herself farther, reaching, reaching . . . She seized it, a used Kleenex, something the cleaning woman had missed. And then—

" . . . I'll see you in half an hour. Well done, Doctor," said Stephanie. Her voice was close—too close!

Dr. Jewel's voice rang back. "Thanks. I feel we'll get a lot of valuable coverage from this case."

"I know you've made a lot of believers."

"I'm only sharing what the spirits tell me. By the way, let's make it fifteen minutes. Can you do that?"

"Sure. Not a problem."

A key jiggled in the lock.

While they'd talked Cameryn had pulled herself the rest of the way beneath the bed, scrunching her knees as close to her chest as she could squeeze them so nothing would show. Willing herself to breathe softly, her heart hammering beneath her ribs so loud she was sure Jewel would hear, she waited. The door opened, then shut with a decisive bang. A shadow that must have been his feet brushed by, the footsteps absorbed by the heavy carpet. She was trapped, alone with Jewel, in his room.

Chapter Fifteen

OH MY GOD OH MY GOD oh my God!!! The words wheeled through her head as she waited, afraid to move, afraid to breathe. She could hear Jewel scrape open a drawer, listened as he flicked his lighter, heard the sound of him sucking the end of the cigarette in small puffs and a long, lazy exhale. Soon, the smell of smoke wafted to where she hid. He kicked off his beaded moccasins, which dropped to the floor with quiet thuds.

The bedsprings protested as he sat on the bed, and she could feel the metal press into the flesh of her arms. *Beep, beep, beep beep,* came the sound of the phone as he dialed. *Beep, beep, beep beep, beep beep beep.* Eleven digits—it must have been a long-distance call.

The bedsprings hurt as they cut into her shoulder. *Don't move!* she ordered herself, even though her arm, the one pressed underneath her body, was slowly going numb. She heard her own breathing as she panted softly through her mouth, and then, conscious of the sound, switched to breathing through her nose. Quieter that way.

"Hi there," Jewel was saying. "I'm calling about a car I picked up from your rental place last week. But I'm sorry to say the way I had to leave it was kinda messed up. Can I have customer service? . . . Thanks." She could tell he was taking a drag from his cigarette. He sighed, tapping his foot as he waited.

His voice had shifted somehow, as though he'd absorbed some of the West's rhythms. And a car rental? That made absolutely no sense! Hadn't Jewel flown into the Durango airport? Hadn't he been driven to Silverton in a limo? Why would he have needed to rent a car? When would he *ever* have needed to rent a car?

"Yeah, hello, Hertz Rental Car? I'm calling because I rented a sweet little number from you on the fourth of the month. . . . Uh-huh, that's right, I picked it up from your airport in Santa Fe last Friday. So listen, I'm afraid I'm all the way in Texas now. . . . Yep, I'm smack-dab in Houston as we speak. I'm calling about the return. . . . Yes sir, I really screwed up getting the Corolla back to you."

Cameryn strained to hear every word. Jewel was lying through his teeth, spinning a tale for someone on the other end of the line. It would be important for her to memorize every single detail.

"So here's the deal," Jewel went on. "I had to catch a flight from Santa Fe today, but I was delayed on the mess of a freeway. Did you know there was a real slow-down this morning? . . . Well, there was. I was delayed almost an hour! By the time I screamed into the airport I knew there was nothing I could do, so I left your Corolla in the airport parking lot. . . . Yeah, I know I was supposed to check it in myself but I'm telling you I barely made it on my flight."

Hertz must have been saying something back, because Cameryn heard Jewel utter a series of grunts. "Uh-huh, uh-huh, but you're not getting what I'm saying. . . . I'm not arguing with you. I'll pay any additional charges you want to stick on my account. . . . Yeah!" He laughed now. "No problem. Just add 'em right on my bill. I rented the car for five days. It's a white Toyota Corolla, license . . . let me see, I wrote it down here. . . . ABD Eight-Seven-Four." Another drag on the cigarette. The stream he exhaled whistled between his lips. "It's in lot three, row six, slot A. . . . Uh-huh . . . Just a few hours ago. I locked it and left the keys under the floor mat—you have a second set of keys to open it, right? . . . Yeah, I thought so. Send someone to the lot to pick it up and turn it in for me."

A beat later, she heard, "That's great, really great. . . . I didn't give it to you already? . . . Man, I must be completely mental from all that freeway crap. It's Jankowski. Raymond Jankowski. J-a-n-k-o-w-s-k-i. You've got my credit card, right? . . . I'll call tomorrow to make sure there was no problem on your end. . . . Yeah, you'll never know how much you've helped. Good-bye."

He must have flicked his ash into what remained of his glass of water, because there was a faint hiss.

Beneath the bed, Cameryn stayed motionless, like stone. She didn't understand what he was doing with the rental car, but one thing was clear: Jewel was a liar. And then, with sudden clarity, she realized, she had the proof that would show he was a killer. The pieces fit like dominoes falling in a perfect pattern, as if they were part of an elemental formula she had to learn in science class. Jewel had hatched a scheme where the car he used in a murder couldn't be traced back to himself. He'd left the rental car—the car he must have used to abduct Rachel— back in the airport lot in Santa Fe, where it sat along with thousands of other automobiles in perfect, anonymous rows. Then, after he called it in, the Hertz people would find it, clean it up, then send it back out into its fleet, never knowing they just destroyed a crime scene. The plan was twisted and brilliant, like the man himself. Lights went off in her head, spinning like a glitter ball, and she could tell she was beginning to hyperventilate again. *Steady*, she told herself.

Jewel began to whistle as he gathered up his belongings. He dropped his lighter and bent down to pick it up. Cameryn's heart stopped when she saw his hand so close

to her, but he picked it up, all the while whistling, not seeing a thing.

She heard a drawer open and shut, then Jewel's voice.
"Front desk? . . . Yes, I'd like the name of your best
florist. . . . Thank you very much." And then, when he'd
dialed the new number, she heard, "Yes, this is Dr.
Raymond Jewel. I'd like to order a special flower arrangement to be delivered to the funeral of Rachel Geller." He
gave all of his information to the florists. "The card?" he
asked. "Yes, I would like you to write down this personal
message from me. 'To the Geller family. Rachel soars with
the angels, but is never far from home. You'll forever be in
my thoughts and prayers.' . . . Yes, and please, sign my
name to the card. Make it a three-hundred-dollar
arrangement. . . . Thank you so much."

Did he have any conscience at all? Cameryn wondered fiercely. He was sending flowers to the parents of
the girl he brutally murdered only days before. She
could barley breathe beneath the bed, the dust was
thick in her eyes, and her stomach felt squeezed into
her throat because the thought of what he'd done, of
what he was doing, sickened her. Of course he had pre-
meditated every angle. Jewel had been in his "cleansing period" right before the murder—Stephanie herself
had said so. She'd also said Dr. Jewel didn't see anyone,
or even eat or drink, which gave him a perfect alibi.
How long would it take to drive from Santa Fe to

Silverton, then back again? Quickly tabulating the distance, Cameryn figured it was no more than eight hours each way. That gave him eight hours to pick a victim and kill her and leave the body. Eight hours to troll the streets of Silverton, looking for the perfect waitress to kill. Back in Santa Fe, no one would have realized he was gone, especially if he played a tape of him chanting in the room for anyone who might listen in. She had no doubt if she took her map with the locations of the other bodies, Dr. Jewel would have had a conference in a nearby state. Far enough away to lessen suspicion but close enough to strike. Her muscles were beginning to cramp, but she didn't dare move.

Jankowski. *White Corolla, license plate ABD 874, rented by Jankowski,* she repeated to herself. She didn't want to lose even the tiniest fraction of information.

And Justin: How could she have been so blind to even suspect him for a moment? Adam, Justin—they were victims, too. "Jewel couldn't have killed her unless he knew how to be in two places at the same time," Justin had told her. Ironically, Dr. Jewel had managed to do exactly that.

Mentally, she counted the minutes. *Breathe softly,* she told herself again. Don't move. Stay still. Her arms were slowly going numb, and she could feel the hexagon of the bedsprings imprinting her skin.

Once again, the bed shuddered, and she watched Jewel's feet, barefoot and only inches from her face, as he stood on the carpeted floor. The feet made their way to the closet. Out came the suitcase, which he placed on the area on top of her. A drawer scraped open and he removed the contents, then went into the bathroom and padded back. Items were placed into pockets and zipped. Through her small slice of sight she watched him pick up the shoes, heard him scrape the hangers across the rod, felt the weight as the suitcase grew heavier. For a moment she panicked, thinking he might check under the bed, until she remembered there had been nothing placed underneath. Just a few more minutes and she'd be safe.

Ten more minutes and he'd be gone from the room, from the Grand. Ten more minutes and she'd be free to tell Sheriff Jacobs everything she'd heard. The alarm clock's *tick tick tick* clicked like a metronome, marking bits of time, clicking away the seconds.

Finally, Jewel zipped up his suitcase. Once more, he opened the drawers, checking to see if he'd left anything behind. Cameryn knew she was almost home free. She could taste it, could feel welling inside her the need for justice for Rachel and for all the other victims. He slipped on his beaded moccasins. Jewel was moving toward the door now, and her freedom was only seconds away. The luggage wheels squeaked as he pulled up the handle from his rolling bag and snapped it in place, and from beyond him she could see a sliver of light in the hallway, back-lighting the fringe on Jewel's moccasins. Another yard and he'd be gone. He was through the threshold now; the door was beginning to creak shut. *Yes!* she cried inside her head as the door inched closed. Her left leg and arm felt like wood but at least now she could move them, and she'd just begun the contortions to free herself when it happened. *Her cell phone rang.*

The *Lord of the Rings* theme song cried out from her jeans pocket in shrill notes, pointing a finger to her and her hiding place, giving her away. *No! No no no!* On her stomach, twisted into a knot of limbs, she tried desperately to grab her phone. *Maybe he didn't hear—the door was shut!* Fumbling, she wrenched her arm around, not caring when the little barbwires scratched through her sleeve and into her bare flesh. She had to get to her pocket. Hair spilled into her eyes, blinding her as her fingers found the cell phone. By feel, she punched off the ringer and waited, watching the door, registering the seconds. *One, two three,* she counted. The door stayed shut. *Four, five, six.* There was no sound now except her own ragged breathing.

Oh, please, don't come back. Please, please, please! Shaking her head, she managed to get her hair from her eyes. She waited, watching the door. Nothing moved. Jewel must not have heard the ring of her cell phone, or he must have attributed it to another source. *Thank God!* she whispered. *Oh, thank God!*

But then the door creaked open again and she saw Jewel's feet rooted into the hallway floor. He stood there for a moment, unmoving. Then he moved inside. The door shut again, quietly, gently, and now she saw the bottom of the suitcase, saw the feet planted into the carpet.

Cursing silently, she watched the edge of the bed ruffle as it hung, shielding her. Her heart was thumping now, frantic, hammering beneath her ribs. There was nothing she could do. She couldn't move, couldn't expose herself, couldn't hide. The breath sucked back into her throat as those feet walked toward her and stopped at the side of the metal frame. *Oh my God!* she screamed inside her head, and she meant it. *Oh my God, help me! My God, please don't let him look here. Let him turn away!*

Light streamed in as the bed skirt flipped up. She heard his knees pop as Jewel squatted down and then his face, seamed and cold, stared at her.

"Hello, Cameryn," Jewel said softly. "Have you been there long?"

She couldn't answer. Fear jammed up in her throat, blocking her words. But even if she could speak there was nothing to say.

"I'm sure you've been there long enough." He maneuvered his arm and from somewhere inside his jacket he produced a gun, small and silver. As he aimed it at her face, she saw the black hole of the barrel pointed directly at her eye.

"I have a permit to carry this. A celebrity like me

never knows what kind of whacked-up crazy'll stalk him. But I had no idea *you* were such a fan. Come on out, Cameryn," he said again. His head dropped to his shoulder as he stared. With a chilling smile he added, "The spirits have a message for you. They want me to get it just right." His eyes fluttered shut for the briefest moment, then opened. "Yes, I got the message," he said. "They say it's time you join the party."

Chapter Sixteen

IT TOOK HER ONLY SECONDS to wriggle out from beneath the bed. She felt Jewel roughly grab her foot, pulling it so hard she thought for a moment it had separated at the ankle.

"Stand up," he commanded.

She rose to her feet, shivering, her brain going a hundred miles an hour as she tried to figure out what to do.

"I'll take that," Jewel said, plucking the cell phone from her hand and dropping it into the pocket of his blazer. He stared at her with an odd expression. Worry creased his brow, although his perfect hair was still in place, combed straight back, with miniature rows left from the teeth of his comb. He paced for a moment, thinking. Finally he waved the gun in her face. "Sit," he said, pointing the barrel to the bed. "So you heard about my car-rental return. Pretty ingenious, don't you think?"

"I . . . I don't understand. I mean, I was under the bed but I couldn't follow what you were doing—"

"I said *sit*!"

She did as he ordered. Her arm and leg were still numb, but the feeling was coming back into them. Once she'd read that when faced with a killer, the victim needed to personalize herself. Talk to the perpetrator, the books said. Engage him in conversation. Making sure to use his name, she said, "Dr. Jewel, you don't want to hurt me. I swear to you I don't understand what's going on. The thing is, Dr. Jewel, I thought you were already checked out. I work for the Grand and they sent me to clean your room. That's all!"

"Drop the act, Cameryn. I'm sure you understood plenty—well, too much for your own good, anyway. But my problem is"—he grimaced—"what am I going to do with you now? I can't let you go and I'm clean out of Christopher medals."

The admission sent a cold shock through her, like a wave of ice water. So there would be no more deception, no veneer of truth covering the lie. Dr. Jewel had just admitted he was the Christopher Killer. She sat ramrod straight, her fists clenching, unclenching. As the reality of the situation hit her hard, her first impulse was to collapse into it. She couldn't let herself. If she did, she would die. *Think,* she commanded. *Think!* But the fact was that he had a gun and there was nothing she could do; there was no way to talk her way out or to strategize. The gun was small, maybe only a .22, but she knew it didn't take much to kill. Helpless as she watched him pace, she began to say the Lord's prayer under her breath.

"*Shut up!*" he snapped. "I'm trying to go over my options, none of which are looking too good at the moment." He ran his fingers through his hair, destroying the sheen. "I was on my way out and now this—you've really put a monkey wrench into my plans, Cameryn. I'm supposed to be out of here in one hour. You look like you have something to say to me, so say it!"

She could only form one word. "Why?"

"Why!" He stopped moving. His eyes widened as he answered, "*Why?* I would think that's pretty obvious. I was a hick kid from a town no bigger than Silverton and look at me now. *Look at me!* I've got everything. I'm on *Oprah.* People listen to every word I say because they think I *know.* But in this business, if your credibility slips"—he snapped his fingers—"you're gone. Done for!" He began to pace again, a tiger in a cage. "NBC was downstairs, interviewing me for the *Today* show. Do you know how big that is? *The* Today *show!*"

The gun was still trained on her, a central point around which Jewel revolved. "My agent's in negotiations *right now* for a whole new show for that network. Oh, I've been on cable, but to take *Shadow of Death* to NBC, maybe even international . . ." He stopped, his eyes sparkling with the thought of it. "We're talking *millions* of dollars. *Ten million* a year or more!"

Cameryn spoke so softly she wasn't sure he could hear her. "So this is about money?"

"What else? Don't look at me like that—like *you* don't have a price," he spat. "No one knows what they'd do until the money's dangling in front of them. I want you to be honest: What would you do for ten *million* dollars? Come on, Cameryn, you can tell me. At this point, you've got nothing to loose. Would you sleep with a man?"

She sat, silent.

"Would you cheat on a test? Would you hurt an animal? Tell me, Cameryn, I'm asking you for the truth. What would *you* do for all that money?"

"I wouldn't kill."

Jewel snorted. "People kill people every day for a buck. What I'm building is an *empire*! I'm famous against all the odds. And I do have the gift," he told her. "I'm really good. But, in this business, good isn't ever enough. There's a pressure you can never understand. A psychic has to be *great* to land the really big deals."

"Rachel Geller had a family who loved her. They all had families."

"I'm sorry about that. Really, I am. But it's been a necessary evil. Look what it got me—Raymond Jankowski, kid from nowhere, ends up on top."

Inside, her heart was beating like mad. "It's *wrong*, Dr. Jewel. I think deep down you know that. I don't think you want to hurt me."

Muscles in his neck pulled beneath his skin like wires. He was standing over her now, and from that angle his features were sharp. "You don't know anything about my 'deep down,'" he raged. "I keep thirty-seven people employed. *Thirty-seven* people! Do you know what kind of responsibility that is? But I do it every day, without complaint. I talk to dead people and I sing for the camera. A long time ago I made a vow to do whatever it took to keep my show going and I've done that. I'll keep doing that."

"By murdering four innocent girls?"

"There are two hundred and sixty million people in this country. Four deaths are statistically irrelevant. I mean . . . five." Jewel rubbed his eyes, then blinked hard. Suddenly, his face seemed to clear, like sun flashing through a stormy sky. His features realigned and he became strangely calm. "There's only one thing I can do. It's time for you to cross over to the other side, Cameryn. You will walk through the valley of the shadow of death."

Panic welled inside her. The man was serious, deadly serious. *"No!"* she cried. "Dr. Jewel, come on, don't do this. *Please!"*

"You took a gamble. You lost. I guess you can go back to saying that prayer now. It's probably a good idea, actually."

Thoughts of her father, of her mammaw and her friends and the mother she hadn't seen blurred together in a kaleidoscope of images. *I wish I remembered you, Hannah. I wish I'd read your letter.* But it was too late. Regret welled in her heart as she thought about what she would never know, never understand. Cameryn had always read that when faced with death, a person's past flashed before their eyes. But it was different for her—she saw the life she hadn't yet lived. How could it all end in a hotel room with faded carpet and a wilting mattress?

"Death is just one small step in a journey. It won't be so bad, Cameryn. Rachel's already there." With his left hand he unzipped his suitcase and felt inside a deep pocket while his right kept the gun trained on her. "Where is it?" he muttered. "Ah, here it is. If you searched my things, and my guess is you did, you never would have thought to look in here." He held up a bottle of vitamins. When he shook them, the container rattled like a tambourine. Setting it on the nightstand, he searched his suitcase again. "Aaand, one more little item . . ." His left hand fished another pocket until he held up a pair of long-nosed tweezers. "I want you to consider this: The reason I've lasted this long is because I'm always thinking. If you want to succeed, you've got to plan. You've got to think it all through from every angle but be ready for anything.

That's what happened when Adam showed up at the end of Rachel's shift. *He* took her home, which was definitely not in the plan. But I followed them. He left her off at the end of her driveway and I just gathered her up, as easy as picking a flower." He poured the vitamins into an ashtray and then, awkward because of the gun, stuck the tweezers into the empty bottle. For an instant she wondered if she should run, but the gun was still pointed at her head and the door was too far. Slowly, delicately, Jewel pulled out a piece of cotton. Then he shook out a handful of small white pills.

"This is my little arsenal. Roofies. I love these things. By the way, I knew all the autopsy reports would list roofies in the girls' blood, which would prove the killer couldn't have been your friend Adam. That's why my 'vision' let him off the hook. I knew they'd have to clear him eventually. Proving once again what a brilliant psychic I am."

Cameryn swallowed hard. "You used the DMSO to get the drugs into Rachel's bloodstream. That's how you did it."

His eyebrows shot up his forehead as he nodded. "So you figured that out. I guess I should have seen that coming," he said with a wry smile. "But, seriously, I'm impressed. Really, I am. Most people don't know a thing about DMSO. Then again, you *are* from the sticks. They use it on horses, don't they? The great thing is that no pathologist ever runs a screen for DMSO."

She watched him fill a glass and drop in two small white pills. "Or have things changed in that department?" he asked calmly. "I have to check out facts like that, you know, to stay ahead of the game. In a way you could say I'm in your business." He swirled the water in the glass and held it high.

Her voice trembled as she asked, "What are you doing?"

Smiling his television smile, he replied, "Making you a little cocktail. I promise, after you drink it you won't mind what I do to you. And I give you my word that I'll make your transition into the other dimension a fast one." He extended the glass to her. "Drink up."

"Are you crazy?" Cameryn recoiled from the glass. "I'm not going to touch that stuff."

He lowered the glass and raised the gun, resting it against her temple. "Perhaps you fail to see the dilemma you're in. You've got no bargaining power. Drink it, or I'll shoot you. Your choice."

The barrel of the gun was cold and her skin twitched beneath it. Terror seized her, but she knew she couldn't let it show. She had only one strategy left. One small, tenuous strategy, as fragile as a butterfly wing. Lifting her chin, she said, simply, "Then shoot me."

Dr. Jewel took a small step back. "Wh—what are you saying?"

"I said shoot me. Go ahead."

"Well," he said, "this is interesting." Eyeing her, Jewel set down the glass. He rubbed his free hand against his jeans, leaving a faint shadow of sweat on the fabric. "I would have pegged you as a girl who would fight to the bitter end."

Adrenaline, mixed with fear, surged through her. "You want me to drink the roofies so I'll be out of it, so you can sneak me out of the hotel like you did Rachel. I'm not drinking it." Her voice shook, so she cleared her throat. "If I have to die, I—I won't make it easy for you."

"So you're sassy," Jewel said, grinning. "You forget, though, that shooting a bullet into your head isn't exactly what I'd call 'hard.'" He picked up a pillow from the bed and placed it between the gun and Cameryn's head. "For the noise," he added.

"You shoot that gun and there'll be forensics splattered everywhere. I'll be all through this room—they'll find me! I'll be on the walls and in the carpet. I'll be on the bed. My blood will be evidence you can't get rid off. They'll know it was you."

"Not to worry. I'll think of something. I *always* think of something." She could hear him cock the gun. Wincing, she squeezed her eyes tight; sucking one last giant breath into her lungs, she began to pray her last prayer.

And then the sound of the door being kicked in. Her eyes flew open; in a blur she saw Justin, his hands in front of him like a diver, his own gun gleaming.

"Drop it!" Justin screamed. "Drop the gun, Jewel. *Now!*"

"I'd do what my deputy says," Sheriff Jacobs added. He stepped into the doorway just as Jewel lowered his own gun. The sheriff held his pistol differently from his deputy—with one arm extended straight in front of him. "Justin here's from New York and the boy's got a temper. Drop the gun to the floor, Jewel. My deputy'd shoot you same as look at you. Fact is, the taxpayers of Colorado would be saved a lot of money if you took a bullet. Our budget's pretty tight this year."

"This girl broke into my room. I—I was just defending myself," Jewel stammered.

"Sure you were. That's why you had the pillow in your hand." His voice became deadly serious as Jacobs took a step closer. "I knew Rachel Geller. Put your gun on the floor or I swear to God, I'll kill you myself."

Jewel let go of the gun as though the metal had suddenly caught fire.

"Kick it to me with your foot!" Justin ordered. *"Kick it!"*

With the side of his foot Jewel sent the gun spinning toward the door. In a smooth motion, Justin reached down and picked it up.

Dazed, Jewel asked, "How . . . ?"

"Dr. Moore sent us," Sheriff Jacobs answered, only he was talking to Cameryn now. "He ran the test for DMSO and got a hit. He tried to call you back, and when you didn't pick up he contacted my office. He told us to hightail it to Jewel's room. I didn't believe you'd actually break in here, Cammie, but Moore insisted you'd be the type to do it. 'Reckless,' he called you. 'And smart.' When we found out the skeleton key was missing we really put two and two together. Looks like Dr. Moore was right. . . ."

Cameryn began shaking violently. Her teeth chattered and her body shuddered all the way down her legs and then Justin was next to her, pulling her to her feet. "Shhh," he said, stroking her hair. "It's okay now, you're safe. Shhh. He can't hurt you anymore."

"Go ahead, Deputy, get her out of here," Jacobs instructed. "I can handle this piece of garbage."

While Sheriff Jacobs cuffed Jewel, reading him his rights in a staccato voice, Justin led Cameryn into the dim hallway. She wanted to stop, wanted to get a grip, but she could only weep—for herself and for Rachel and the other three girls who'd lost their lives at the hands of the monster. She'd come as close to death as was humanly possible, and lived. She couldn't absorb that fact, couldn't make sense of it. A moment before, she'd been preparing to die and yet here she was, alive again.

"Are you okay?" Justin asked. His brow creased as his eyes searched hers.

It was hard to speak, but Cameryn managed to choke out, "I'm all right."

He brushed a lock of hair from her face. "Is there anything I can do for you?"

"Yes," she answered. Wiping her face with the palms of her hands, she took in a deep, wavering breath. "Take me home."

Chapter Seventeen

"I THOUGHT JUSTIN WAS the killer. I really did. That's why I went to Jewel in the first place. When I saw that *M* on Justin's license plate . . ."

"It's all right, Cammie," her father replied. "There might be some psychics who are real, but many of them are frauds. The fakes throw out numbers or letters or whatever and let *you* find the connection *for* them, you see? Practically everyone has some random connection with the letter *M*, or any number of letters or sequences of the two. My first girlfriend's name was Miranda. It's an old trick."

They were on the swing, with Cameryn resting her head on her father's shoulder. She pulled back so she could look at him full in the face. *"Miranda?"*

"Let's not get off subject," he replied, so she settled back in to him. She pushed the swing with her foot and it began to move again, rocking her comfortingly.

"What bothers me," she said, "is that I knew about that stuff and I still fell for it anyway."

"You and millions of others."

His arm was around her, strong, protective, and Cameryn marveled that the day's end could be so different from its beginning. The evening air was cool, so she nestled in closer, and when she did he kissed her roughly on the side of her head.

"So, after all this, do you still want to be assistant to the coroner?" he asked.

Cameryn paused and let the motion of the glider, which creaked beneath her father's weight, carry her three passes before she replied, "Ask me tomorrow."

"Oh, believe me, I will. I want you to stay on. You're smart, Cammie. We would never have caught Jewel without you. You stopped Jewel from killing again."

"Smart?" She almost laughed at this. "First I thought Adam killed her, then Justin—I don't call that smart."

"Well now, don't be so hard on yourself. Jewel fooled a lot of people. Sheriff Jacobs called me and explained how he was able to cover his tracks with his rental-car scheme. He'd go into that—what did he call it?"

"Cleansing period."

"Right. Cleansing period. Anyway, he used that time for his alibi. And guess how he got out of the hotels unnoticed?"

"How?"

"Wearing plain workman's clothes. Wearing the cap and his old glasses that distorted his eyes, no one even registered him."

"I saw the clothes but I didn't make the connection." Cameryn found the hangnail that was bothering her and bit it.

"Don't bite your nails, Cammie."

"I wasn't—okay, I'll stop." She dropped her hand into her lap, while Patrick went on.

"Just think, a big celebrity like that and nobody saw him. He rented the car for a week but left it in the airport lot, then checked it in by phone. That was the genius of his plan."

Looking up, she said, "I'm not sure I really understood that part of it."

"The police checked him out every time there was a murder. But they knew Jewel had to get from point A to point B, right? So they'd look into all the flights out of town and every rental-car place, seeing if just maybe he'd rented one and left town. The police knew he was making speeches the day *after* each murder. So they were checking for cars that would have been returned by then. They could never find one that fit the bill. Until now."

Cameryn thought about this. "I'm glad Jewel's talking. At least now the families will have closure. Did he ever say why he used a Christopher medal?"

"Because he was raised Catholic and I think a bit of it still clung to him in a warped way. He killed while he traveled. He told the detectives he thought he was death's patron saint. What a sick, screwed-up man."

"Who said he talked to dead people. You know, from now on I'm going to stick with science. When I'm a forensic pathologist I'll use only the facts."

He squeezed her tight and said, "Except you were using a bit of intuition there yourself. Which makes you a natural for the job." He reached out and playfully caught Cameryn's nose between his knuckles. "Although I don't know why we're talking about your future when you're grounded for life—"

"I thought you just said I was fantastically intuitive!"

"You are. But, bottom line, you could have gotten yourself killed." His voice thickened as he craned back his neck to look at the stars. "You're all I've got, Cammie. In this whole wide world, you're all I've got. Promise me you'll never take such a stupid risk again."

As she nodded, her cheek rubbed against his shirt. "I promise," she whispered.

For a while they sat silent, content to glide. Overhead, the aspen shivered in the wind, creating a sound like the rushing of water. The currents began to blow, first in ripples, then in waves, and she marveled how the wind passing through leaves could conjure the rumble of a distant ocean. She, too, dropped her head back; like her father, she gaped at the sky overhead. Silverton was small enough that the town itself cast almost no light, so the space above her was black as ink, studded with tiny, brilliant lights. Looking into the endless deep of space, as thick with starlight as the ocean was with plankton, she thought how it was like looking at life upside down. Her own life, too, looked different, a reverse of what it had been. Only days before, her mammaw had accused her of being too dark. Strangely, she didn't feel dark any longer. She'd almost become a body on the autopsy table, an object to be opened up and read, sewn up and buried in the ground. To be alive, to have another chance at tomorrow, was a wonderful thing.

The wind surged again, harder now. Shivering, she pressed deeper beneath her father's arm.

"Dad?"

"Hmmmm."

"Hannah's trying to find me."

His grip tightened so hard she winced. "I know it."

"I want to talk to her. When I thought I was going to die, that was the one thing I was sorry about. I was sorry I never gave her a chance. I was sorry I wouldn't read her letter."

It took a long time for him to speak. "You don't know what you're asking. You don't understand."

"That was okay before—not understanding—but not now. Dad, I want to get the letter."

"Your mammaw already has it."

As if on cue the porch light flicked on, flooding the backyard with light. Above, the stars faded, but she could see her father now, though his eyes were still shadowed.

"Are you warm enough, you two?" her grandmother's call carried over the grass. "Don't answer that—I don't even know why I'm asking. You'll say you're fine when you're a breath away from freezing. I'm bringing out a blanket."

Her mammaw, standing in the strong porch light, traveled carefully across the lawn. Stiff, she stepped on flagstones, her body rocking with off-center weight from the thick quilt she carried. When she reached the swing she unfurled the blanket, tucking it snugly beneath Cameryn's chin.

"Lyric called and I told her you'd call back. She and Adam are going out, celebrating, but I took the liberty of telling her you'd be staying home tonight. You've had enough excitement. What is it, girl?" She felt her grandmother's strong hand on the top of her head. "What's wrong? Patrick?"

"You've got my letter," Cameryn whispered hoarsely. "From Hannah."

The smile slowly drained from her grandmother's face. "I do," she said.

"How did you get it?"

"The deputy came by. He gave me two things. A letter and a package."

"I want them."

"Patrick?" Mammaw asked, but he didn't answer. That seemed to be answer enough, because Mammaw said, "I'll go get them."

Time stopped. Her grandmother was gone only moments, or was it hours? Cameryn couldn't tell. Patrick stared straight ahead, unmoving, his eyes wide and blank. When her grandmother returned she pressed two objects into Patrick's hand. "The child's right," she said softly. "Tell her."

But her father shook his head. "No. Not yet. I'll do it tomorrow."

"Son, if you've learned anything from today, it's that we don't always have our tomorrows."

"I need more time," he said. His mouth had been the only thing to move. He did not meet his mother's gaze or his daughter's, but stared into the darkness.

"No, Patrick," she said softly. "I've heard every argument you've come up with as well as a few out of my own mouth, and the both of us have been wrong. It is time. You've got to tell her the truth."

Then her mammaw caressed Cameryn's cheek with her hand, pulling her chin up so that their eyes met. "What we've done—it's been from love. We've always tried to protect you."

"I don't understand."

"You will." Mammaw turned and made her way back to the house, her fuzzy slippers padding on the stone. The screen door screeched open, then went silent.

Suddenly Cameryn's blood began to race. She stared at the package, wrapped in iris blue paper, then at the letter, encased in a plain blue envelope. Her father made no motion to give them to her.

"Dad?"

"It's strange, the way we've been sitting here, talking about death." His voice was oddly flat, and when his eyes met hers, he didn't seem to really see. "About death, and dying, and ghosts." He swallowed. "There are different kinds of ghosts. When we moved here, Cammie, I wanted to forget. They were things about Hannah, about our life before, that I've never wanted you to know. I thought it was better to bury the secrets. To forget the past."

"Dad, what is it?"

Her father took a deep, wavering breath. "Cammie, you don't remember everything. About who you are, I mean. It was too long ago. But . . . there's another person. . . ."

For some inexplicable reason her father had begun to cry, yet, strangely, he made no sound. His face contorted while quiet sobs shook his body, rocking the swing with spasms. "I'm sorry, I'm sorry. . . ." he said in a hoarse whisper. "I can't do this." He stood. With a final, wavering breath, he let the package, then the letter, slide from his fingertips into her lap.

"Do what you need to do," he told her. Then he walked, unsteady, following Mammaw's footsteps along the flagstone that made a path toward home.

Cameryn was left alone. Rocking, feeling the breeze, she tried to steel herself for this new reality. Because the porch light was so bright she could no longer see the stars, but she could see the pines, waving their arms as she stared into the heavens. Turning over the package, once, twice, she let it drop back into the blanket, then picked it up again. She hesitated only a moment before she ripped off the paper. Inside was a picture. Two girls, maybe only three years old, had been painted in soft watercolor. Two dark-haired little girls in pink dresses with smocking, laughing, their mouths wide. Cameryn saw herself in the face of them both. It made no sense. Hesitant, she picked up the letter. It felt light in her hand, as fragile, as inconsequential, as a leaf. The envelope was made of pale blue paper; when she looked closer, she saw the watermark of an iris.

Somewhere, an owl hooted and she heard a rustle in the grass behind her. It was probably a mouse about to get caught by the owl, an animal that could find its prey in the dark. A part of her was like the mouse, running and hiding, but a bigger part was like the owl. She'd been searching for something all her life and she sensed it was right here, in the blue envelope.

She didn't give herself another chance to think, afraid she'd change her mind. Trembling, she tore open the envelope and removed a single page.

Cameryn unfolded the letter she'd waited all her life to read. It was written in black ink that swirled across the paper like bits of lace.

> My darling Cameryn,
> I love you. I want to say that in case you don't read another line of this letter. But I love you more completely than I have ever loved anyone before or since you came into the world.
> I realize that you must have always had questions about me—why I left, why I chose to disappear from your life. But death can make a person walk a path she never thought herself capable of. In my grief, I ran away from you. Now, I realize what a mistake that was, and worse, that it might now be too late.
> Cammie, when your sister died,

a piece of me died, too. Jayne's
death sent me to places that were
not safe for you. But now I'm
well again.

Stunned, Cameryn looked at the picture. Jayne? She had a *sister*? It was impossible. Cameryn would have remembered, would have known . . . wouldn't she? The smiling face of twins stared back, mocking her with their silence.

I'm asking you, begging you, to
contact me. If you call me I'll
know you're ready. There's so much
to say, Cameryn, so many years to
fill. Please, I won't care about
the hour. Day or night, you can
always find me.

Beneath the scrolling signature she saw a phone number and a New York address. Above her, the owl glided, his wings spread wide to embrace the evening. She read the letter again and again. Then, hesitating, she pulled her cell phone from her back pocket but didn't open it. At that moment the owl swooped in on its prey and flew up into the night. The mouse's tail hung from its talons like a velvet cord. It was already dead.

Death. She had wanted to serve the dead, wanted to learn their language so that she could be their translator. She remembered thinking how much of her life had been buried with Hannah's memory and how cordoning off her past had stolen her own voice. But for the first time Cameryn understood it was the secrets themselves that had silenced her. And they'd silenced Hannah as well.

Once again the pines trees danced overhead. Rousing herself, Cameryn flipped open her phone and dialed the number written on the bottom of her letter.

The letter from her mother.

Acknowledgments

I'd like to thank the many people who helped me explore the forensic field. You have unselfishly shared your knowledge and passion—the glimpse into your world rocked mine! I'm especially grateful to: Thomas M. Canfield, MD, Fellow at the American Academy of Forensic Sciences, Chief Medical Examiner, Office of Medical Investigations; Kristina Maxfield, Coroner; Robert C. Bux, MD, Associate Coroner, Medical Examiner; Dawn Miller, Deputy Coroner; Werner Jenkins, Chief Forensic Toxicologist; Chris Clarke, Forensic Toxicologist; Sandy Way, County Coroner's Office; and a special thanks to Scott Short, D-ABMDI Deputy Coroner—without whose help this book would not have been possible.

Keep reading for a preview of
the next Forensic Mystery

THE ANGEL
OF DEATH

Chapter One

"DO YOU KNOW how many laws we're breaking?" Cameryn Mahoney demanded.

Deputy Justin Crowley shrugged nonchalantly. He was driving his Blazer with one hand draped lazily over the wheel while the other brushed back his too-long dark hair from his eyes. "Well, if I had to guess, I'd say at least six," he answered slowly. A smile curled at the edge of his lips, making a kind of comma in his cheek as he added, "Maybe more."

"Six laws. And this doesn't worry you?"

Another shrug, only this time his shoulders barely moved. "Not particularly."

"*Why* does this not worry you?"

"Because there's a dead body on the side of the road, which can't stay there. That's a fact. The sheriff and the coroner are out of town, which is also a fact. That leaves the two of us—Silverton's trusty deputy and its extremely capable assistant to the coroner"—he nodded in her direction—"to work the scene. In other words, it's just you and me. And we're doing it."

"This is crazy. *You're* crazy."

"Just doing my job."

Trees whizzed past as Justin downshifted around a hairpin turn on the Million Dollar Highway, a narrow two-lane road that ran like an umbilical cord from tiny Silverton all the way to Durango. To Cameryn's right, Colorado's San Juan Mountains towered above her in a granite block, while to her left the mountains fell away in a thousand-foot sheer drop, a yawning mouth of a valley bristling with Engleman spruce beside streams with fluted ice as thin as parchment. According to Justin, there was a body on this road that Cameryn was supposed to process, without tools or a gurney or even a pair of latex gloves. Messing up at the beginning of a case could mean disaster if it ever went to court. They shouldn't even think of processing a scene alone. It was insanity.

"You're chewing your fingernails again," Justin pointed out. He glanced at her for the briefest second, and in the relative dimness of the car's interior his eyes looked more green than blue, the color of a lake reflecting evergreens. "What are you so nervous about? I thought you liked this stuff."

"I *like* being prepared and I—this—this is all wrong. We should radio the police in Durango or Montrose. Or something."

"*Relax.* You've been so uptight lately—did you know that?"

"We were talking about the remains, Justin, not about me."

"All right, all right, back to the case. There's something funky about the body. All I'm asking for is your quick, professional opinion and then . . . boom." He hit the heel of his hand against the steering wheel. "You're outta there."

The seat belt cut into her neck as she twisted to face him, protesting, "But I'm *not* a professional. How can I give a professional opinion when I'm still in high school?"

"Ah, but you've got to admit you know more than I do," Justin replied. "You're a forensic guru. You're so good that—guess what Sheriff Jacobs calls you when you're not around! Come on, take a guess."

Cameryn closed her eyes and groaned. She knew what was coming. A quip, a sly remark about her working with the dead—she knew folks in Silverton whispered about her all the time, under their breaths, their words falling like snowflakes only to melt beneath her resolve. It didn't take much time with the living to remind Cameryn why she wanted to be a forensic pathologist. The dead didn't tell stories, except about themselves.

Although Justin seemed to register her groan, there was no stopping him this morning. "Jacobs calls you the Angel of Death." The deputy grinned as though he'd just given her the highest compliment. "What do you think about that?"

She replied with her standard answer, the one she always gave, her Pavlovian response. "I'm into the science of forensics, not death."

"Tell it to the sheriff. *I'm* not the one who gave you the name." His eyebrows, dark half-moons, rose up his forehead as he smirked. "Angel."

Another hairpin turn, only this time a huge semi-truck roared up the mountainside, belching greasy smoke into the morning air and leaving a gassy trail behind.

Like a vapor winding its way through the streets of Silverton, the idea that she loved death had dissipated throughout the tiny town of seven hundred citizens and had crept its way through the halls of Silverton High. It encompassed her friends, who squirmed at the fact that she'd seen the insides of a human body. It drifted over to her boss at the Grand Hotel, who made Cameryn soak her hands in bleach water before setting the tables, something he never asked the other servers to do. Her own grandmother, whom she called "Mammaw" after the Irish way, clucked whenever Cameryn read forensic books, convinced that the mere study of those books would somehow condemn her soul to hell. But her father, the real coroner of Silverton, encouraged her. "You've got a talent, Cammie," he'd say. "You *see* things. What you have is a gift."

The blinker's staccato clicking broke into her thoughts as Justin pulled onto a dirt overlook. He pointed expansively across the highway. "It's over there," he said, "behind that big boulder."

"You keep calling the body an 'it.' Is the decedent a male or female?"

"Hard to tell. Our little animal friends did quite a bit of chewing on it. That's not what's bothering me, though." He turned the key, and the engine coughed and died. "I think the best thing will be for you to see for yourself."

"I can't believe I'm doing this."

"Come on," he said. "Check it out."

Beyond the dirty windshield Cameryn saw a partial mound on the left side of the road, smaller than she'd expected, although the entire shape was impossible to discern from her angle. She got out of the Blazer and hurried behind the deputy as he crossed the highway. The lip of the road was narrow on the east side, the ground uneven, treacherous with rocks and roots. Beneath her, the faraway trees looked as though they were set in miniature. She slipped on a layer of faded leaves pooled at the trunk of a tree and made slick with melting frost, but Justin grabbed her elbow to steady her.

"Careful," he said.

Panic whined inside her because she knew she shouldn't be here. Maybe there was still time to call for help. . . .

"It's right there," Justin said, gesturing with his free hand.

Beyond the rock, rising like a half-shell, was a body, shadows dappling the surface of what looked to be the remains of a small person. The sickly sweet smell of decay filled her nostrils, but she ignored it as she moved closer, her heart drumming with nervous energy. Something was happening; it was as though a switch inside her had been thrown. Now the clinical side, the science part of her brain, pushed to the forefront, drowning out the objecting voices. Suddenly she wanted to see the body and examine it. There was a puzzle here, and it was possible she could put the pieces together to learn its secrets.